SCREWBALL

SCREWBALL

by Alberta Armer

ILLUSTRATED BY W. T. MARS

THE WORLD PUBLISHING COMPANY

Cleveland and New York

F
Arm

Published by The World Publishing Company
2231 West 110th Street, Cleveland 2, Ohio
Published simultaneously in Canada by
Nelson, Foster & Scott Ltd.
Library of Congress Catalog Card Number: 63-8914
4WPHC1066
Copyright © 1963 by Alberta Armer

To Austin and Rollin,
my two mechanical geniuses

Contents

SCREWBALL

My First Coaster

Just suppose you were a twin. I am, and I tell you, sometimes it's no fun. For one thing, you're compared to your brother all your life. This is all right if you are the good one, the strong one, the big, husky twin like my brother Patrick. I'm not. I'm Michael.

People call me Mike, but they always use Patrick's full name. He greets everyone with a wide smile full of white teeth. He is good at any game, and he never reads a book through to the end. He just says, "You tell me how it comes out, Mike," and goes out to play baseball in the empty lot. He's usually head of his team, too.

If you want to know what I like, it's junk. You heard me, J-U-N-K. It comes in empty lots in Detroit just as baseball games do, but it is quite different from baseball. *Junk*, in case you don't know, is a word for things that have been used and may be used again, even if for something else. There are no rules except that you pay the junkman a price for anything you take away—unless he throws it in with something you've bought.

My favorite junkyard in Detroit is on Livernois Avenue near Eight Mile Road. Livernois Avenue is pretty important in my story. But before I tell you about it, I will have to go back to the farm where Patrick and I were born, because there is where my trouble started.

Being the smaller, weaker twin may sound like plenty of trouble to you. But how would you like it if besides that you got polio before you were even three years old?

In those days farm people couldn't do much for polio. They would have if they had known how. But they didn't know. They even called it by a different name, a long one—infantile paralysis. My mother says those were the two most scary words she knew.

Patrick didn't get it. And my mother didn't have much time to help me get back to walking, because she was busy with our new sister Betsy.

I'm glad only one of us had it. But why did it have to be me? And if it was going to cripple me, why didn't it do a real good job instead of just twisting the muscles of my right arm and leg? Other kids all thought I was just naturally awkward—"crazy," they said sometimes, or "screwball."

When I was about six my Dad bought me a pair of roller skates to make my legs stronger. He told me to practice on the strip of concrete sidewalk lined with flower beds that ran from our front porch to the highway. I tried for hours to learn to skate. When I tried to stand up on those wheels I'd fall down. Then I had to hold onto the steps to pull myself up. But it wasn't any good. As soon as I was standing straight again, my feet would shoot out from under me. I must have sat down on that sidewalk two hundred times the first day.

Then Patrick came along and said, "Let me try." He put on the skates, gave himself a shove to stand up quick, and skated away down to the gate as if he had been born on wheels. After that I wouldn't try again.

But I did like wheels all the same. So I sat on the doorstep in the sun and spun the wheels of one skate around with my finger. I could hear the ball bearings tumbling inside. I peeked in and saw them nudging the axle. They shone like silver.

When I got tired of playing with the skate I lay flat on my stomach and looked between the cracks of the porch floor. Down there in the cool and the damp I could see sow bugs.

I crawled under the porch and touched a bug with my finger. It curled up tight.

"Look," I called to Betsy. "Here's a new kind of ball."

Betsy laid down her doll and came under the porch too. Sunlight through the floor cracks made slanting stripes across her cute face.

"Ooh, Mike," she said. She touched a bug and it rolled up. She carried it up the stairs and rolled it along the porch floor.

I kept bringing her more bugs to make into balls. The biggest one we called the Father One, and we rolled him back and forth between us. We had to be careful not to squash any, because a dead bug will not make a ball of itself.

I had a wonderful idea. I went to Dad's desk and got some paper, a soft lead pencil, scissors, and a bottle of airplane cement. I made a little oblong paper box, turned it upside down, and drew windows on both sides. Then I dropped it over The Father sow bug.

"Look," I said, "it's the school bus."

The Father Bug began to crawl along the porch. He looked like a tiny school bus on its way to pick up the kids and take them in to Manton Joint Union School.

Betsy laughed till I thought she might choke. I always could count on Betsy to like my ideas, just as I always knew Patrick would shake his head and say, "Screwy, real screwy."

A day or so later I had a bigger idea. I took the wheels off one of my roller skates and bolted them to a wooden box just big enough to hold Betsy's doll. I bored a hole in the front of the box and tied on a piece of heavy twine. It made a dandy wagon.

Betsy pulled it into the kitchen, where Grandma was watching a story on television about some people who went to California in covered wagons.

"Look, Grandma!"

Grandma peered. "Oh, Mike, my dear, your nice skates. It's too bad you took one apart."

I knew I wouldn't be scolded by my Dad and Mom though. They always went sort of easy on me, since I was the puny one in the family. If Patrick had taken one of my skates to pieces, he'd have heard about it, for sure. But there was something respectful about the way my folks scolded him, as if to say, "You're a fine big strong boy. You can shoulder a lot of blame, but

Mike can do what he wants to because we're sorry for him." I'd got so I didn't mind this too much. And sometimes I took advantage of it.

Grandma's TV show gave me another idea. I got Dad's pliers and cut up one of Mom's coat hangers. Then I bent wire loops over the top of the box with Betsy's doll in it; and this made a covered wagon. Grandma gave me an old handkerchief to stretch over the wires.

When Dad saw the covered wagon that night he laughed and said, "I give up. I'll never buy you any more roller skates."

"You sure ruined them," said Patrick. "They're nothing now but junk." I could tell he was mad and felt I should have been punished.

The days on our farm were long and good without much happening. We lived on a hill looking down on the little town of Manton. Behind the barn the old orchard tilted up against the sky. Here apples grew every summer into green balls striped with red.

Beyond the farm were cut-over hills, with burned stumps and little trees where there had once been forests. In the valleys were small, round lakes where our friend Butch and Patrick and I caught bluegills on summer mornings. Fishing was always fun. I was as good at it as anyone, and the fish didn't know any difference between Patrick and me. Butch kind of preferred me because I sometimes made up stories or told him about Tom Sawyer while we walked home with our fish.

Everywhere was space and quietness, except on the

farm where the things I liked best all made a noise—the tractor, the mower, the cream separator, even Mom's sewing machine. Patrick often played catch in the barn lot with one of our cousins; the socking thud of the ball in his leather glove was as regular as the chug of Dad's tractor—the "johnny-pop," we called it. Betsy chased chickens and caught them just as they tried, squawking, to get under the barn. Dad primed the pump to fill the reservoir on the stove, and it went *scree-eech* for a while till the water came. That kind of noise.

Dad went with Patrick lots of times after supper to the ball park. He would have taken me too, but I said I didn't like ball games. This kind of hurt my father, I think, so he and Patrick went off alone. When my twin got into bed with me later, his hands usually smelled so buttery with popcorn that I could hardly go back to sleep.

But Dad took *me* when he went to Smitty's Garage in town. Something was always going wrong with the pickup or the tractor. He would drive it to Smitty for advice. Then I could hang over the engine while the two of them talked it over. Dad never cared if I got grease on my hands and clothes.

He had been an auto mechanic himself when he was young. He had married my mother during the war and gone to work for her father on the farm. Then Grandpa died and Dad was sort of stuck there taking care of the place, and his mother came to live there too. But he never really took to farming except for the mechanical parts of it.

I could tell how he felt when he took me to Smitty's shop. It was like home to him. Automobiles and motors and mechanical gadgets were what he liked best. And me too!

Smitty's walls were hung with gaskets and rubber tubing and coils of wire. There was a wire cage over the electric-light globe. It was on a cord that he could pull to any place in the garage. There was a good clean smell of gasoline all over that room. In front of his garage Smitty had a Model-T Ford with a brass radiator shell. He used to tell me that if I'd come to work for him some day, he'd let me polish it every morning.

Smitty kept his blue shirt sleeves rolled above the heavy muscles in his arms, and he could fix any motor. He'd tinker and tinker till, finally, it began to purr. Then he and Dad would look at each other and grin and nod their heads. Smitty was always good-natured. I guess any man is good-natured if he knows he can do what he's expected to do.

One day I was fooling around the tool shed on our farm. This shed leaned against the north side of the barn, and moss grew in bright green patches on the old red paint. It was so full of worn-out tools and machinery parts we couldn't close the door. That shed is where I got my first love of junk. Boy, we had it!

I found a set of wheels, part of the baby buggy we three kids had all ridden in. It was a twin buggy, so I guess Betsy had had an awful lot of room. It was almost hidden under a phonograph with a horn shaped like a morning glory. I pushed it out into the barn lot.

"Look," I called to Betsy, who was eating grapes

under the back porch. "These wheels are almost like new. We could take them off and make a coaster. Isn't that a good idea?"

"Oh, yes, let's, Mike." Betsy hugged her elbows.

I got Dad's wrench and a screwdriver and took off the front and back axles. Then I went into the barn to hunt for a board. Sunlight came through cracks in the walls, and millions of grains of dust danced in the brightness. I felt as though fingers were pointing at me as I pulled a loose board from the top of Nellie's stall.

In the woodpile I found a couple of two-by-fours and nailed them crosswise under the long board for axletrees. I drove nails in a straight line in each two-by-four. Then I laid an axle from the baby buggy close to the row of nails, and pounded each nail into a hook around the axle, front and back.

This was my first coaster, and I was as proud as any mother hen with a fresh new yellow chick. I rolled it back and forth in the dirt. Betsy crouched on her heels and looked on.

Here came Butch, eating a cold cob of corn. He looked it over and spit out a piece of cob. "Say, that's not bad," he said.

We took it to the top of the orchard. Grass grew in a thick fuzz between the apple trees and made a good slick track. I had not thought of a way to steer, and at first we kept bumping into trees. Then we found an opening between two rows of trees straight down to the barn lot. Down this we rolled till suppertime, yelling like Indians.

Patrick came home from playing ball at our cousin

John's. "We won. Our team won the game," he called, and washed his hands and face at the pump. But neither Betsy nor I even answered him. We had a coaster, and I had made it myself.

When Dad saw the coaster, I was both proud and ashamed. I knew that I should be able to guide the front wheels, but I did not know how. And Patrick said I should have asked for permission to take the baby buggy apart.

Mom looked at the baby buggy frame I had pushed aside in the dust. "How much money do you have in your bank?" she asked, real cross. "You'll have to pay me fifty cents apiece for those wheels."

"Okay, Mom." I liked the way my mother never made me feel like a worm. She just made me pay up.

Dad scratched his head as he walked around the coaster. He didn't really look mad. "Come on," he said suddenly. "We'll go to the lumberyard and get a new board to put on Nellie's stall. You pay for that. But I'll buy you a carriage bolt."

"A carriage bolt? What for?"

"I'm going to show you how to make a steering front axle."

So that's how I learned that a carriage bolt could make a coaster steer. First Dad made me pull all the nails from the front two-by-four and lift off the axle. Then he drilled a hole down through the body board and the crosspiece and another through the axle. Down went the carriage bolt through all three holes. And on went a washer and two nuts at the bottom.

Now the front axle could turn on a pivot. I sat down on the board and put my feet on the ends of the axle. If I pushed with my right foot, the wheels turned left. If I pushed with my left foot, the wheels turned right.

"Swell," I said.

"Let *me* try," said Patrick.

"To steer it right," said Dad, "we'll put a rope from one side to the other. Then you sit way back and steer with the rope. Pull on the side you want to turn toward."

Dad found some rope. Later, I had to laugh when Mom came out of the kitchen and scolded, "Someone has been at my clothesline and cut off a big piece. Whoever did that will have to pay for it."

"Dad did it," shouted Patrick. I was surprised at his voice, as if his throat was thick with tears. Now when I think about it I know that he must have minded it that my ideas were always taken so seriously. He was so strong and healthy that no one worried much about him. My folks were glad he took to baseball and was out all the time playing with his team. Naturally, it must have hurt him the way they made a fuss over me.

I couldn't see this then, but since what happened in Detroit I've been giving it a lot of thought. You know, I used to feel sorry for *myself*—when all the time I should have had more sympathy for Patrick.

He was the one who always caught the blame if we didn't get back in time from a hike. Mom would be impatient with him. "Why didn't you start home before dark?" But she never scolded me that way. It was as if she was just glad I was alive.

So I know how Patrick must have felt when he took that coaster out into the orchard after dark and began coasting down between the trees. I don't say he meant to wreck it. But he couldn't have been watching where he was going when he crashed into a tree behind the barn.

Dad was doing some figuring under the reading lamp, and the rest of us had just turned off the television set when Patrick limped through the back door.

One knee was skinned, and there was a long scratch

down his leg. It was beginning to bleed, thick and sluggish, through a lot of greenish bruises. He was brushing dirt and twigs off his shoulders and trying not to cry.

I must admit I thought first about my coaster. The front axle was bent, and one wheel turned at a crazy angle. Dad had put on the back-porch light and I could see he was half mad and half worried.

First he looked Patrick over and said in his worst voice, "Go to your mother. Ellen, help him clean that cut." Then he turned to look over my coaster.

Honestly, it seemed to me that Dad felt that ruining the coaster was even worse than having Patrick hurt himself. And I know Patrick realized how Dad felt too. I saw the look he threw me when he came out into the barn lot after Mom had cleaned his leg and bandaged it.

Dad was examining the axle and finally he said, "We can straighten it, Mike—almost as good as new. But you be careful you don't do what Patrick did . . . crash into a tree. Crazy business. Never should have taken it out after dark."

I felt sorry for Patrick. He did so like to be thought well of. It wasn't that my folks loved him less. They were terribly proud of him. It was just that the love they felt for me always hurt a little bit, I guess.

Good-by, Farm!

Making that coaster is the thing I remember best out of our twelve years on the farm. There were some bad times when the place didn't make enough for Dad to pay the bills. He said we were land-poor—too much farm and not enough equipment. We never had enough money for trips to the city like Butch's folks and like my Uncle Horace and Aunt Suzy, who had the farm next to ours.

I'd never been farther from Manton than Higgins Lake where we sometimes went in summers to a cottage we owned. The year I was twelve, Dad went to Detroit in August, and I was mad because he didn't take us along. Later, I knew he'd gone to look for work.

One day he came in from a trip to the post office, waving a letter. "We're going to move to Detroit," he said. "I've got a job in an auto factory. How about that, Patrick, how would you like to go with me to watch the Tigers play?"

"Oh, boy, Dad, and maybe—can I learn to bowl?" yelled Patrick.

"Sure. And Mike and Betsy can go to libraries and museums."

Dad didn't mean it to sound as if I were a sissy. I knew that. But I didn't like the way Patrick laughed, loud and horsy.

Grandma shook her head. "You all go if you want to," she said. "I will not move from this farm."

"I've talked to Horace," Dad told her, "and he's agreed to farm this piece along with his own. You can stay right here. They'd rather move into this house than be in their own. This is bigger."

It was very exciting news, and Mom's cheeks were bright.

"We have only a little while to get ready," went on Dad. "I have to be at work in two weeks, and school will start the week after that."

I must have pulled a long face, because Dad said, "You'll like it, Mike. Millions of cars. Detroit makes more cars than any other city in the world."

"Will we take the pickup?"

"Yes, but I plan to trade it in on a car as soon as we get settled."

Dad was sitting by the kitchen table lighting his pipe. Betsy put down her doll in the covered wagon she still used and climbed onto his lap. Betsy was the cutest kid; I wish you could see how she looked, sitting there, leaning back against Dad's chest. She was ten, but she still had faint dimples in the backs of her hands at the knuckles; and she had a habit of using one fore-finger to curl the little tails at the ends of her shiny braids. Her eyes were brown like Patrick's and mine, but merrier somehow, tilted a little at the outer edges.

"Betsy will have a whole new set of friends," said Dad, giving her a squeeze.

That was easy enough to believe. She always made friends everywhere. Give her ten minutes and she'd find someone to get acquainted with.

All the things I had never thought much about became important in the next two weeks.

I camped once more with Butch in his father's cornfield. We carried blankets between the rows of dry, rustling stalks, with grasshoppers flying out at us in clicking, dust-colored clouds. We dug a hole and made

a fire in it under a sheet of rusty iron, and roasted wieners. We watched about a billion stars come out in the dark blue above our heads.

"Can you find the Little Dipper?" said Butch.

"Sure. It's over there, right above the city dump."

"Remember how we learned to shoot there, Mike? Dad set up a row of tin cans on the edge of the dump and we shot 'em down with our twenty-twos."

"Sure did."

"Is it true, I wonder, that you can hear corn grow at night?"

"I don't know. Keep quiet; let's see."

We listened but didn't hear a thing.

"Too late in the season," said Butch. "Look, there's the Big Dipper with the handle pointing right down at your barn."

"Yeah. I wonder where it'll point when I look at it in Detroit."

We crawled inside the cornstalk tepee we'd made, rolled up in our blankets, and slept a few hours. Early in the morning without a word to each other (our teeth were chattering) we woke up and crept through the pale air back to our own beds.

Patrick and I went fishing one more time in our favorite stream, hidden from the road by willow trees. We left the house before the sky was light, cramming our pockets with bread and cheese. At the compost heap behind the barn we dug enough fat night crawlers to fill the tobacco cans in our pockets.

The brush at the edge of the brook was so thick we could hardly force our way in to get our hooks into the winking water. Willow stems snapped up into our faces and slapped us from behind.

Before the others were up, we were back with trout for breakfast. "Patrick caught five and I got twelve," I said boastfully. "But mine are all little," I had to add.

"The little ones taste best," said Grandma.

Each time I fed the animals now I wondered how I would feel when we had left them behind—old Nellie; the two cows; Shep with his long hair full of burs; and pigs, cats, and chickens whose numbers no one knew exactly.

Uncle Horace came over and Dad took him all over the place. Then they signed some papers in the kitchen.

One night I woke up and could hear Mom and Dad talking in the dark. I didn't mean to listen, but at night when all the farm noises are gone, and before the roosters start, it's easy to hear voices.

"I wish when we get to Detroit Mike could turn over a new leaf," Dad said. Of course, after that my ears were sharp.

"Why?" said Mom. I knew that tone of her voice, as if she felt people had a right to criticize me but she wished that they wouldn't.

"Well, he's alone so much. Always tinkering. Fooling around. Never joins a team. Doesn't even try to play games."

"You know why, Frank. He doesn't like to be made fun of, and he is awkward. And he likes other things that are just as important."

"Like what?"

"Well . . . could Patrick have made that coaster?

Does Patrick care to see how the tractor works? Or does he gnaw his knuckles when something goes wrong with the machinery around here?"

"All the same—"

"And who remembers all about Huck Finn and Old Mother Westwind and Mowgli?"

"Ellen, now listen! You know Mike would be happier if he mingled with other boys more—"

"There's Butch."

"Yeah. Butch he's known all his life. But I'm wondering how it will be in a new place."

I pulled the covers over my head and made a solemn resolve: "I will turn over a new leaf. I will mingle with other boys." Then I felt better and went to sleep.

Now there was one more important thing to do before we moved to the city. That was to visit our cabin on Higgins Lake.

"I'll have to fix a few leaks in the roof and put new locks on the doors," said Dad. "Next summer Horace will have to take care of renting it."

It is only an hour's ride to Higgins, a clear, spring-fed lake among tall pines. Our cottage looks like a log cabin, but the chinks are filled with cement so it's waterproof. There is a long screened porch on the lake side, and in the sand around the cabin are huckleberry bushes.

Dad and Patrick mended the roof and I put the new locks on. I am much handier with a screwdriver than Patrick is. Mom and Betsy aired out blankets and cleaned away mouse tracks.

Early next morning busy little sandpipers were running along the wet sand close to the lake. I could see them from my bed on the porch. They were still in deep shadow, but when I looked up at the pine trees the top needles glistened like jewels from the rising sun. Then I saw that Patrick's bed was empty.

When I got up he was already coming out of the lake, dripping from a cold swim. He might have called me. I wasn't such a bad swimmer. That was one thing Dad had insisted on, because water sports were supposed to be good for my muscles.

Higgins Lake is clear everywhere. If you stand still long enough in shallow water, you may see the shadow of a minnow move right over your foot. When you wade in you can see your toes on the bottom, all the way out to the diving raft.

There's an old rowboat at our cottage. I could never row very well because of my darned right arm. But by turning in circles a good deal I rowed Betsy out to the water-lily bed that morning. In the hot, still air the lilies smelled like fresh cookies.

We leaned over the sides of the boat and caught hold of lily stems as slick as snakes. Betsy pulled so hard that her face turned red. She is a very stubborn kid. She leaned far over the side of the boat and plunged her arms into the water, tugging and grunting.

But the lilies were more stubborn. The stems slid out of her hands, and the lilies bobbed on top of the water as if they were laughing at her.

"Look," she said then, "a water snake." We watched it make a jagged path through the water, its head tilted to the surface. I reached out my hand, but the snake

darted away among the big round shadows of the lily leaves.

When we got back to the cabin Patrick said, grinning, "Where you been? The bakery truck came and the man would've taken you into town with us. I got a chocolate soda at the drugstore."

"I don't care," said Betsy. But somehow I did. Why could Patrick make me feel that drinking a chocolate soda was better than trying to catch a snake among the water lilies? That's the way Patrick has always been. Even when he isn't superior he makes you feel that he is.

On the last afternoon Dad said, "Well, the cabin is ready to rent now. Let's catch some perch, kids."

Dad rowed far out into the lake. The water was calm, without a ripple. When I peered down into the lake I wondered how far I could force my glance into that bottomless green. Somewhere down there were hundreds—maybe thousands!—of fish.

"Ought to be good fishing time, just before a storm," said Dad. He could always tell when a storm was coming up. His pipe made little sucking noises in the quiet. The sun came down warm on our backs below the shadows of our straw hats.

Finally far down in the shadowy green world something told the fish that it was time to eat. I felt a tug on my line, but I never can believe it when a fish first takes hold of the bait. I waited, wanting to be sure.

Dad said quietly, "Got one," and made an arc of his pole, bringing in the first perch. He was so busy getting the hook worked loose that he didn't see me struggling. This was a big one; I could tell by the fight it put on.

Patrick saw me fighting it and right away decided I needed help. I could have landed it alone; I know I could. He stumbled across the bait can and grabbed my pole to bring a big fish to the surface. This upset my balance and over I went into the bottom of the boat, where I flopped among the worms, and, now, the fish that Patrick had landed with my pole.

"You had to pull in *my* fish," I yelled, sore as a bear. "You h-helped me because you weren't having any l-luck."

"That's a beaut," said Dad, helping me to my feet. "Be quiet, Mike. You want to scare away the rest of the fish?"

It was not as big as I had thought while I was fighting it, but it was an inch bigger than Dad's. Even though Patrick didn't get any on his own line that afternoon, I couldn't forgive him for catching *my* fish! You know what I mean?

The storm hit the lake about four o'clock, and it was scary. The water turned all shades of blue like a crazy quilt. Waves looked bright purple on one side and the color of a robin's egg on the other. Lightning cracked the sky, kind of like a knife hitting an egg, and white-caps moved fast toward the shore ahead of our boat.

A big wind blew and rain was lashing the pines when we scraped bottom. "Patrick, help me pull the boat up on the sand," said Dad, "so it won't drift out. Mike, you carry up the fish and the bait cans."

"I can take the poles and the oars too," I said crossly.

We cleaned the fish on the back porch. A ring of neighborhood cats formed at once to get the guts and heads. We could smell the kerosene stove and frying bacon. Patrick didn't say a word about not having caught any fish on his line and helping me with my big one; and believe me, neither did I.

After supper Dad and Mom played cards with the neighbors. When we kids went to bed on the porch, we could smell Dad's pipe and the other man's cigar. The storm had worn itself out, and on our faces we felt the breeze flowing in from the lake.

I often remembered all this after we were settled in Detroit. It was a pretty good time, before I knew what homesickness was, before I ever dreamed of playing hookey from school.

The last few days on the farm went fast. Dad had all kinds of business to take care of. Mom filled barrels with dishes and glasses. There were boxes of books and Dad's tool chest and his bowling ball.

I watched the pickup filling and I was worried. Patrick had seen to it that his bat and glove and his stamp book were aboard. I had packed my books and a box of treasures—a snakeskin, a bird's nest, a little imitation Coke bottle, and a tray of mounted butterflies. But most of all I wanted to take my homemade coaster.

At last Dad made room for it on top of a box of Grandma's quilts. "Now, Mike," said Grandma, "don't you take up with any city slickers."

"No, Grandma." I wondered what a city slicker was.

"I kind of wish you were going to stay here with me, boy," she said. "City's no place for a boy like you. Patrick, yes, but not my little Mike." She shook her head and I wondered what she meant. It made me mad, but no one could stay sore at Grandma. She was too old.

On the last evening I went to say good-by to my best friends—Butch; Mr. Loftus, the town undertaker, who owned a 1914 Stanley Steamer; and Smitty.

"Come back next summer," said Smitty, wiping his greasy hand on a rag before he took mine. "Maybe you can work for me. I'll let you polish the brass on that Model-T out front."

"Okay, sure, Smitty."

I walked once more to all the spots that had been important: the city dump, the junkyard full of old car parts, and the place on the river where I had first killed a snake. The sun had set when I went slowly up the hill to home.

I turned and looked back down at the little town. The lights had come out in all the windows and seemed brighter than the stars.

Dad woke us up at four, and I could smell ham and hot biscuits. When I looked out of the kitchen window I saw the bright circles of my coaster wheels in the back of the pickup.

Shep sat between Patrick and me, begging for rinds of ham.

Suddenly I was homesick! I don't know if you've ever moved from a farm to a big city, but you get most homesick just before you leave. I got up and ran out to the barn.

I was in Nellie's dark stall patting her long nose and exchanging glances of love with her when Dad came out.

"Come on, son," he said, "we want to beat the morning traffic."

I Try To Turn Over
a New Leaf

Betsy sat in the high pickup seat between Dad and Mom. Dad had fixed Patrick and me a pallet of bedcovers in the back. We pulled some of the covers over us and rode backward, looking straight up into the sky still polka-dotted with stars. They were getting dimmer as the light came up in the east. Mom had told me the stars were millions of light years away from us, but they looked close and like friends to me.

Patrick went promptly to sleep. I looked down at him, envying him the ability to go to sleep so quickly. Watching him was a little like looking into a mirror except that his face was broader and heavier than mine. His hair was my shade of light brown but more sunburned—a kind of gold—around the temples. There were, I guess, seventeen or more freckles on his short nose. I laughed when his wavy upper lip twitched in his sleep. He must be dreaming he was telling someone off—maybe me! His lashes were dark and his brows were straighter than mine. But if you've never been a twin looking at your brother asleep, there is no use trying to tell you about this.

"Now," I said, looking right at the North Star that I knew I would see the longest, "I'm going to turn over a leaf when we get to Detroit. I'll join a ball team and learn to play so Dad will be happy and proud of me. I'll make lots of friends . . . I'll mingle."

By and by I too fell asleep.

Almost two hours later I woke up and saw that the sides of the highway were crowded with houses. At the edge of the road were little tents with signs reading, "Tiny red fishing worms for sale," and "Night crawlers and grasshoppers."

Sure seemed funny that people would have to *buy* worms! I began to think the city must be a very strange place. I sat up straight and leaned my back against the pickup cab.

There were stores now, and buses stopped at corners where people were waiting. Men and women were hurrying along, crowding each other in the streets. They all looked pretty much alike, rushing in all directions like fish in a hatchery. Sometimes a used-car lot or an automobile showroom went by before I got a good look at the cars.

Dad stopped at a tiny house about the size of the Manton Ice House. A blackboard in front said: "Good homes near schools. Stop in."

A tall stringy man came out chewing a toothpick. "How do. You folks want to look at houses?"

He took us to a street with wide smooth lawns, where sprinklers were like fountains everywhere. Brick houses looked down among trimmed shrubs, and huge shiny cars stood in driveways.

"Oh, no," said Mom. "Can you imagine us in one of those places? We want something more . . . well . . . like us."

"I know what you mean, lady. A two-family flat?"

We drove up a street with narrow two-story houses on both sides. Each house had a double driveway, a lawn about the size of a handkerchief, and an upper and a lower porch. Above every high-peaked roof stood television antennas.

The man stopped his car next to an empty lot, in front of a house that had been painted white but now needed its face washed. The doors had been scratched by pets "wanting in," and scooters and bicycles were lying on what had been a patch of grass. Boys were playing baseball in the lot, and girls sat under a wild cherry tree watching them.

The man jingled his keys. "There's an upstairs flat empty here, and the Pontchartrain School is in the next block. The next main street is Eight Mile Road."

The game stopped for a minute, and I could feel the boys watching us climb the back steps. They were sizing us up. The man unlocked the door and stepped back for us to enter. The whole flat could have been put into the kitchen on the farm. I could not believe my family was going to live in such a tiny place.

But Betsy raced through the rooms. She skated on the shining yellow floor and shouted, "Can I have this room, Mom?" She came up to me and put her hand in mine, saying gaily, "Oh, Mike, don't you love it up high? It's like heaven."

She ran to a window and looked down at the boys in the lot. "There's a boy at first base with red hair," she reported.

I looked at all the little bare rooms. "But there's no furniture," I said. I had never thought about furniture not coming with houses. I felt a queer dull pain at the strangeness and smallness of everything.

Dad went with the man to sign some papers. And Patrick—? You guessed it. He went right downstairs to watch the ball game. By the time Dad drove the pickup into the driveway later, a plump blond boy was talking to Patrick. Even from where I watched at an upstairs window I could see they were chummy already.

The new boy came over and opened the garage door for Dad. His trousers seemed about to slide off his hips, and he kept hitching them up. He was so plump he was almost fat. "I'm Jimmie Hoyt," he said. "We live in the flat below you."

"How do you do? I see you and Patrick already know each other. Have you met his twin?"

"Twin?" His voice squeaked with surprise.

"Yes." Dad called up the back stairs, "Mike, Betsy, come help me unload." When I came down Dad said, "Meet your new neighbor, Jimmie Hoyt."

"Hi." I felt like a little dog being sniffed by a very large one. I wished I'd come down right away like Patrick instead of having to be called.

There was no room in the garage for my coaster.

There was barely space for two cars, with a shelf for cleaning supplies. The backyard had clotheslines in parallel stripes above it and flowers along one fence.

Dad handed down the coaster. "There must be a place to keep this in the basement," he said.

I followed him into a cool dark space. A big furnace

spread asbestos-covered arms in all directions. It reminded me of a picture of an octopus I'd seen once. There was a coal room and there was laundry space, and along the inner wall near the furnace was a long workbench.

"Maybe you could use that," said Dad. "We'll ask

the Hoyts. Anyway, you can keep your coaster underneath."

I thought of the tool shed at home bursting with wonderful junk, but I said, "This is nice." I went and stood under the wild cherry tree watching the ballgame. I saw too late that I was among a lot of girls. I should have joined the boys behind first base.

"Wanta play?" called Jim Hoyt.

I shook my head. "Not—not today." I couldn't turn over a new leaf all at once. Patrick looked as if he wished he were not related to me.

I carried armfuls of books and blankets upstairs while Patrick took his turn at bat. Mom and Dad were too busy moving in to notice much. Mom did call, "Patrick, why don't you help now?"

But Dad said sharply, "Oh, let him get acquainted, Ellen. Mike, *you* don't need to help us."

"I want to," I said sullenly, stumbled, and almost fell down the whole flight of stairs.

Betsy found her ball and jacks and played on the downstairs porch, where she was soon joined by a girl she later told me was Charlotte.

Dad and Mom made trips to grocery and furniture stores. The first night we spread our mattresses on the floor, and we drank milk out of the clover-pattern china cups with little bits of straw floating in them. We couldn't heat anything till the gasman came. So we ate cold beans out of cans and made quick store-bread sandwiches.

"Like a picnic," said Betsy happily.

I thought of real picnics on the Manistee River. I

remembered throwing meat scraps to Shep and skipping rocks across the water with Patrick and Dad till the sun went down.

How do you know when the sun goes down in the city? I wondered.

Next day I still did not want to go downstairs, so I watched the furniture men distribute the new things around the square rooms. I knew already what it is like to be really homesick.

Patrick and Betsy went down every day in the week before school began and came up to report on new friends. "Charlotte taught me to play Russian hand-ball," Betsy said. "She has a brother and sister with red hair, Hubert and Mildred Lucile McMurtrie."

"Yeah, I know." Patrick made big muscles in his arms, first one, then the other, feeling them as if he didn't know I was watching. "Mildred Lucile wishes she could play ball like us boys."

"She's got a case on you," said Betsy, smiling.

"I know."

"Larry Winslow has big brown eyes like aggie marbles," Betsy said next day. "And there's a kid named Richard Depew who shakes his hair like a pony tossing his head."

"Larry and Richard want me to join the Little League," said Patrick. I didn't need to ask what the Little League was. We had one even in Manton.

"Jimmie Hoyt keeps asking why you don't come down and play ball too, Mike," he went on kindly, like the lordly big brother in story books. "He's a nice guy, Mike."

Finally I said, "I'll come down today and give the little kids a ride on my coaster, the ones who aren't playing ball."

"Oh, your old coaster," said Betsy. "All the boys here have new bikes, or at least scooters. That coaster isn't much."

Well, that shows how much my plans to turn over a new leaf came to. It takes more than a resolve made to yourself to buck a line of new boys when you know in your heart that you'll never make a ball player.

Worst of all I missed my Dad. He'd always been around the house on the farm, or just over the hill in the orchard.

"Run take Dad this pailful of coffee," Mom would say, handing me the pail and a sack of doughnuts she'd just made, all hot and floury-looking with powdered sugar. I'd stand watching Dad eat and drink while the sweat gleamed on his forehead and arms.

Here in Detroit Dad worked hard and long hours, and came home all fagged out, carrying a tin lunch box that held only a pint thermos of coffee and a few sandwiches and pie. When he got off the bus at the corner he looked discouraged and glum. (He said it didn't pay him to drive the pickup to work, but I think he was ashamed of it.) And after supper he'd get cleaned up and take Patrick off bowling somewhere. There was no use taking me. I couldn't bowl for sour apples.

He didn't want to talk with me about mechanical things any more. "I get enough of that on the job," he said one night when I asked him to explain how some piece of machinery worked. "Let me alone, Mike."

I could see I wasn't going to like Detroit much. I even thought once about putting a few things in a bandanna, tying it to a stick, and hitching back to Manton—where I could go to school with Butch. But I knew I'd be homesick for my folks. Anyway, I could never do anything that desperate.

"Screwball!"

I didn't know it at the time, but during that one week before school started I met all the kids who were to be important in my story.

Hubert McMurtrie and Jimmie Hoyt took up with Patrick as thick as thieves. Mom laughed and called them the Three Musketeers while she passed out fresh hot cookies to them with both hands. They are all big and eat a lot and wouldn't be caught dead reading anything except the funnies.

I figured that Larry Winslow and Richard Depew were a little more like me. But they were all so bitten by the baseball bug and so wrapped up in Little League stuff that I didn't have a chance unless I could learn to play too.

There were a lot of others kids on our street, but those five (including Patrick) were pretty much the whole show. When I came downstairs a few times to watch the fellows play, a little guy named Dickie Fells fastened onto me. I dragged Dickie around the block

pretty nearly every day and was actually glad to have
something to do besides just standing around.

Girls, of course, are important too. So I sized up
Mildred Lucile, Hubert's older sister, and decided she
wanted to run everything; that's probably what made
her skinny. She'd been sick, so she had to repeat the
seventh grade, the one Hubert was in. Emmy Jo
Thompson squealed whenever anyone made a homer,
and laughed a lot all the time. She thought she was
pretty cute, and she was. My sister Betsy was the best
of the bunch. I always did think so, even in Manton.

Next to her came her new friend Charlotte, Hubert's
little sister. I began to like Charlotte a lot. She didn't
say much, but once when someone knocked Dickie Fells
down in the sand she helped him up and took him home
to put something on his skinned knee. When I looked
at her sometimes she was looking at me. That makes a
fellow feel real good.

The day school started, Patrick went early with
Jimmie Hoyt. "I'm a Deputy Boy," Jimmie said, "and I
think they might put you on another corner. The boy
who used to stand on the corner across from me—John
Breen—moved away this summer."

"What's a Deputy Boy?"

"You direct traffic, keep the little kids from being
killed. Traffic in Detroit is awful. The school picks the
big boys for the job, one to each corner. We get to wear
white Sam Browne belts and hold Stop signs. When it
rains or snows we get white slickers and rain hats." I
could see he felt important, and right away Patrick did
too, even before they chose him to do the same job.

Hubert called from the street and away they went, the three of them.

I started off with Betsy. Mom gave me a quick hug around the shoulders because she always knew when I felt left over.

The closer we got to Pontchartrain School the more I felt as though it were staring at me with its dozens of windows. The square brick building and playground took up a whole block. Across from the school there was an empty lot full of sassafras and young oak trees. I wished I could be in there among all the green things.

"I'm scared, Mike," said Betsy. I took her hand and squeezed it, feeling better myself.

At the corner Jimmie Hoyt in his white Sam Browne belt held out his Stop sign across my chest. He blew a whistle when it was safe to cross the street. I saw Patrick at the corner across from him; but Patrick didn't look at me.

"How come they took Patrick on right away for a Deputy Boy?" I asked Jimmie. I'll admit I was jealous. . . . Here was my twin all dressed up in a uniform the very first day of school.

Jimmie laughed. "Well, John Breen had that corner last spring and he's moved to Ohio or someplace. Patrick is just his size."

"He sure gets the breaks," I said.

Inside the big front door of the school Betsy darted down the hall to join Charlotte. By the time I found the seventh-grade room my head ached from the thundering noise of new shoes on hardwood floors.

The teacher sat at her desk with her eyes on the door.

Boys and girls came in quietly and found seats as far away from her as possible. She had blue eyes that did not smile, and she held a ruler with which she kept tapping her right palm.

Somehow Patrick had finished his job and gotten there ahead of me. He sat across the aisle from Hubert, looking at Emmy Jo.

I found a seat in the row by the windows. I wished again that I had tried harder to be friends with these kids. Hubert and Mildred Lucile looked cross and nervous and scrubbed. Richard Depew smiled at me across the aisle and so did Larry Winslow, who was small and as neatly built as a seal. But Jimmie Hoyt did not smile. He still treated me like a new dog on the street.

"Here is a list of the subjects you will study and the rooms where they are taught," said the teacher. She began writing neatly on the blackboard. "I am Miss Goodfellow." She wrote down her name too.

I thought of the school at Manton, where I had known everyone. Even the teachers had been my friends, though they often scolded me for daydreaming. Right this minute all my old friends were probably gathered around the piano with the middle C that stuck. And Miss Graham was very likely pounding out, "My country, 'tis of thee," and nodding her head for the kids to sing louder.

Suddenly I heard the voice of Miss Goodfellow. She sounded mean and smiling at the same time. "Well, well, so this boy thinks he need not answer when I speak to him."

I felt my face getting red. "I . . . I . . . didn't hear you."

"I asked you why you weren't writing down the list of subjects and rooms."

"I—I didn't know we were supposed to."

"Did you think you could learn them by heart?"

"I guess I didn't think."

"You guess you didn't think. Well, start thinking. What's your name?"

"Mike—I mean, Michael Williams."

"All right, Mike—I mean Michael." She mocked me perfectly. "Suppose you write that list right now."

There was a piece of yellow paper and a pencil on every desk. I've never been able to write neatly, but with Miss Goodfellow peering over my shoulder I felt like a chicken scratching in the dirt.

When I finished she took up the paper and held it out to the girl across the aisle. "What do you think of that?" she demanded.

The girl giggled. "I can't read it."

"Well, I hope Michael can."

I could see the smiles around the room. Everyone was grinning except Patrick. I made fists in my pockets.

"You all noticed the boys in white belts at the corners this morning," said Miss Goodfellow. "They are there to tell you when you can cross the street safely. We call them Deputy Boys, or Duty Boys. The traffic is so bad that these boys may save your lives. So be sure you cross only at the corners.

"We have a new one this year, Patrick Williams. He's

taking the place of John Breen, who moved away this summer. Stand up, Patrick, so they can all see who you are."

Gee, I hurt way down deep inside. Why couldn't I ever be the right twin? I saw Emmy Jo Thompson look admiringly at Patrick and then whisper something to Mildred Lucile.

A bell rang and Miss Goodfellow said, "Well, that's the first bell. We will just have time to start our English this morning. Emmy Jo, what is a verb?"

While Emmy Jo was trying to think what a verb was, the second bell rang. At once the thunder of heavy new shoes began again. I hung back until the others had scrambled out of the room, then followed them without really wanting to.

By then everyone had already disappeared. I looked out of the front door and saw the trees in the lot across the street.

It was easy, so easy, to slip out and run into their friendly shelter. I forgot about not crossing the street except at corners. I hardly knew I had run away until I felt the quiet green of the trees all around.

I walked slowly into the lot, deeper and deeper, away from the school. Leaves were green hands that reached out on all sides, hands grasping light. Each tree and plant in the lot seemed to have arranged its leaves to get the most light possible.

I picked a jewelweed and carried it like a small friend in my hand. Orange flowers hung like stockings from a delicate stem. A tiny vine, so thin it could never have lived alone, had twisted itself around the stem, growing upward. Under one of the leaves of this vine sat six fat aphids.

Everything depends on something else, I thought.

A spider was spinning its web between an elderberry bush and a hickory tree. It played out the thread from its body, going from stem to stem. Soon there was a perfect pattern. The spider saved the two main diagonals, the anchor lines, for its own runway. All the other lines it made with a sticky fluid to catch insects.

How does a spider know the way to spin one kind of line for itself and another kind for its victims?

I waited, as tense as the spider, for it to catch something. A blue-tailed dragonfly darted among the leaves and was caught in a corner of the web. It beat its way out very fast, tearing a big hole.

Only another spider could know what that spider was thinking! It wound up the web in a kind of hand-over-hand motion with its two front legs, the way I've seen Mom take down a clothesline. It began patiently to rebuild its web.

Then I heard the school bell ring for recess.

" 'Bye, now," I said to the spider. "Guess I'll try it again." I ran back to the schoolyard, past all the children around the Good Humor truck.

When I bumped into a teeter-totter, I stumbled and fell on the cinder yard. Dickie Fells, the littlest boy, helped me up, but I could hear older boys laughing.

"What's the matter," called Jimmie Hoyt, "can't you see where you're goin'?"

"Mind your own business," I shouted.

I know now Jimmie had just been waiting for an excuse to fight. He made his fists hard and danced forward, jabbing me in the stomach before I could brace myself.

I struck back with my left arm. I knew enough to keep my weak right side protected. I'd watched Patrick sparring with Butch often enough. Jim brought a quick uppercut to my chin, and that's all I remember for sure. He couldn't have struck me more than half a dozen chops before I was down. Then he fell on top of me with a grunt.

Well, you couldn't blame Jim. I suppose he didn't know I had had polio. He may have thought I was "uppity."

He straddled my body and turned my head sideways, pressing my face into the cinders. My nose began to bleed.

Jim was tired of this already; it had been too easy. "Had enough?" he asked.

I turned my head from side to side, saying No. I could see the other guys in a ring around us, shutting off the view in case a teacher should see us fighting. I was gulping tears and blood, breathing hard.

Then I heard what I dreaded more than anything— my brother being good to me. "Get up, Hoyt," Patrick said in a real cool voice. "Mike's got a weak right side. He had polio once. Leave him alone."

Jim's hands came away from my face and he scrambled up, brushing himself. "Well, why didn't he say so?" he said in a low voice.

In the hall the school nurse pulled me into her office.

She was a round little woman, shaped something like Grandma's pincushion. She cleaned dirt out of my skin and put stuff that stung on all the cuts. She stuck bandages here and there.

"You sure started fighting first thing, didn't you, Kiddo?" she asked. "Now run along to class."

Room 18 was full of a kind of nervous quiet when I

opened the door. I slid into a seat and saw too late that
Jimmie Hoyt was behind me.

"Where were you when we had arithmetic?" Jim
asked.

I pretended not to hear him.

"In social studies," said Mr. Whitman, "you will learn
about your great city, the automobile center of the
world. Once it was Fort Dearborn, a stockade on a
rapid river."

He pulled down a map of Michigan and pointed out the Upper and Lower Peninsulas. His voice had a soothing sound, and pretty soon my mind went away and wandered in the cut-over hills around Manton.

At last it was noon. I found Betsy waiting for me outside the door. We both had to wait at the corner till Jimmie said it was safe to cross. I looked over at Patrick again, using his Stop sign as if he'd been doing it all his life. The lucky stiff!

The afternoon went better at first. There was chorus for the whole school in a big auditorium full of warm yellow sunlight. Charlotte McMurtrie stood in the alto section, and I looked at her to learn her face by heart. She was small and freckled with a pink nose and fly-away brown hair. She must be very smart to sing alto.

She looked right at me across the other singers and smiled. My heart felt funny, as if it had turned over.

For the last period all of us boys trooped to the gym. There stood Mr. Duffy in a sweat shirt, with the words Pontchartrain School written on his big chest. His eyes sparkled bright blue, and his face was round and rosy. He had a halo of white hair around his head and a little bit of fuzz above his forehead. By half shutting my eyes I could imagine that Mr. Duffy was a cherub, just a round beaming face with a pair of little fluttering wings below.

But when he spoke he didn't sound like an angel. "First we study, then we play," he said. "Every boy here must be good at some kind of sport. Maybe you can't play ball." He seemed to sneer, and the boys horselaughed. "Well, then I'll teach you how to fight."

I thought Mr. Duffy was looking right at me and all the boys were too. But maybe I imagined this. "And if you can't fight," ended Mr. Duffy, "you can always be on the tumbling team." Now the boys roared. "And don't forget, boys," he finished, "I'm the truant officer too, so watch your step."

We spent the class hour being shown the equipment and going over the rules of basketball. I began dreading the next day when everyone would find out I couldn't shoot a basket. And it was plain I was too short to make a decent guard.

I walked home alone. But when I came to the baseball lot Jimmie Hoyt called, "Hey, Mike. You want to bat? Come on, we need another guy."

I figured he was trying to be nice to me, and I could see out of the corner of my eye that Patrick looked nervous. My stomach felt like a concrete mixer with gravel churning inside. Now the kids would see me at my very worst. Any other boy winding up to throw a baseball looks like a beautifully running piece of machinery, but I'm nothing but a jumble of elbows and ankles.

"Okay." I took the bat from Jim and went slowly to the plate while the other kids took their positions. Richard Depew was pitching.

The first ball was a perfect one, over the plate. I swung the bat blindly, missed the ball, and spun completely around, sitting down in a tangle of arms and legs that just could not all be mine.

Oh, how they yelled and laughed before I could get to my feet! I was so mad the tears were pouring out of my eyes, and I didn't even care. When you're so mad you cry and don't mind crying, boy, you're some mad.

"What a screwball!" yelled Jim. The others took up the cry, "Screwball! Screwball!"

I threw the bat as hard as I could throw it. It landed with a hollow cracking sound as I ran across the driveway into the basement.

Behind me Jim shouted, "What a lousy sport!"

But Patrick quickly yelled him down: "Come on, you guys, play ball!"

I Play Hookey

Next morning I dressed and ate so slowly that Betsy ran off to school ahead of me. By the time I got to the corner the Deputy Boys had left their posts. I had planned it that way; I didn't want Patrick to see me. Then I ran into the empty lot across from school.

I didn't feel very wicked about playing hookey. No one had ever said, "What a bad boy!" about Huckleberry Finn when Mom read us that story. Instead, the whole family had laughed and sat around eating popcorn and begging, "Go on, read another chapter." The only trick in playing hookey, I thought, would be to keep other boys from seeing me disappear among the trees. What would be the end of this I didn't know; but meantime, here was this lot full of young trees and underbrush. And I hid there the rest of the week.

I thought of all kinds of ways to pass the time. Sometimes I was an Indian stalking an enemy, creeping along so that no twig snapped. Then I was a naturalist making notes on bird life. I watched a nuthatch run very fast down a sassafras trunk, picking out bugs from

59

the bark. I looked at a hawk high up in the blue and wondered if it could see the little bird.

I spent one morning making a fort in a patch of sand, breaking twigs into even lengths to make a stockade. Then I made even smaller twigs and built houses inside the stockade. I dug a river channel past it, and said to myself, "Fort Dearborn. I wish Detroit looked like this now."

Under a mass of Virginia-creeper vines I found some junk I was sure I could use—bedsprings, the hood of an old Ford, and a roll of chicken wire. I pulled the vines well over the pile to hide it, and came back that evening after supper with my coaster to get the chicken wire. The workbench was mine now; the Hoyts had said I could use it. So I stowed the wire underneath.

By Friday, after a whole week of playing hookey, I had to admit that I was getting pretty bored with that empty lot. I wasn't like Huck Finn after all. For one thing, I didn't live near a river to float a raft on. If I had, everything might have been different. And I was getting worried now because Patrick had noticed I wasn't in my seat in homeroom. The first time he mentioned it I said I hadn't felt well and had gone to the school nurse's room to lie down. That got by; he probably didn't care much.

What I didn't know was that each day Miss Goodfellow checked an attendance sheet. My seat wasn't near Patrick's and he might not have noticed that every day I was missing. But on Thursday she asked him if I was still sick, and that night at bedtime he tackled me about it.

"You been up to something?" he asked in a scolding tone. "You watch out for Mr. Duffy if you've been playing hookey. He asked about you too today."

Sooner or later you always have to face the music. That is a law for boys. I wondered how Mom and Dad would feel when they found out. To tell the truth, I even worried about how Patrick felt, because twins are close, very close. Sometimes, if you're a twin, you wish you could turn your back on the other one, but you can't. It's as if he were part of you, and together you make one boy.

Hiding among the trees on Friday morning, I waited for the noon whistles to blow. Wild grapevines climbed over elderberry bushes all around me. I could smell the flat purple bunches as sweet as little pies in the warm September sunlight.

When the whistles blew I thought of Dad opening his lunch box, along with thousands of other men at the automobile factory. I wished I could be there with him. Gosh, I missed Dad those days when I played hookey!

Now the bells in the school were shrill, and even over here across the street and deep in the empty lot I could hear doors opening, the wild thumping of shoes down halls, and the clang of locker doors. The Deputy Boys raced to their corners. Patrick was quickly slinging his Sam Browne belt into position and buckling it. Kids poured like marbles out of the building, running along the sidewalks and spilling over the edges.

I waited until they had all gone past. When I slipped out of the trees and ran home no one saw me.

After lunch I sat on the edge of my bed until it was time to pretend to go back to school. I held my treasures in my hands, trying to get back a feeling of being myself—the imitation Coke bottle, the snakeskin, the bird's nest, and a box of sinkers, fish hooks, and empty shotgun shells. But they meant nothing here in the city.

"Time to go, Mike," Mom called.

This time I did not go back to my safe hiding place but turned to go in the opposite direction.

When you try to get away from yourself you can walk for miles without noticing you are tired. I zigzagged from one street to another until I was lost. But when I got to Livernois Avenue I decided to follow it.

I had always had a strong sense of direction at home. I knew every little lake among the sandy hills, and I was the first one in the family every spring to find the place where pink arbutus flowers smelled sweet under last year's leaves. On a night of no stars I could find my way back to the farm by the shapes of the hills.

But city streets meant nothing to me. Along Livernois Avenue the stores crowded thickly. No one noticed me at all.

I could smell wieners cooking in a quick-lunch shop and wished I had some money in my pockets. In a beauty-parlor window a plaster hand stood on its wrist, holding up fingers that seemed to be dipped in blood. I wondered if Betsy would ever use that stuff on her fingernails—or Charlotte. In a store where millions of used magazines were stacked, a phonograph was playing a song I used to hear on the radio in Smitty's Garage.

Then something tight eased up inside me, for suddenly I came to a whole block filled with rows of old cars. Streamers above the cars said in big blue letters, "USED CARS—LOW PRICES—COME IN."

I went straight across the gravel yard to a battered black car, feeling all warm inside as if I had found a friend. These cars looked like the ones around Manton, not gleaming with factory newness but dusty and worn with the miles of Michigan. I patted a front tire, bent over a crumpled fender, finally got down on my hands and knees, and began inspecting the chassis.

"Hey, you! You crazy kid, what you doin'?" said a gravelly voice.

I jumped up and slapped the dust from my knees.

"What's 'a matta, kid, why ain't you in school?"

The voice was kind, so I looked up into a plump tan face with bulging brown eyes. The fat lips talked around the edges of a big cigar. "Y'ain't playin' hookey, are ya? Maybe been to the dentist or something, hey?" He gave my shoulder a playful shove.

I backed away and without a word began to run down the street. My neck and ears burned.

At the curb an old man with red-rimmed eyes mumbled something, and I remembered Grandma's words, "Don't take up with any city slickers." I still wondered what one was.

Then I forgot my troubles completely, for here was a showroom full of bright new cars. The front car stood on a Lazy Susan platform that turned slowly, so I could see every dazzling bit of it.

And next to this stood a little racer with a body

painted in black-and-silver checks. It was not a racer for a man but the neatest kind of toy for a boy like me. I could fairly feel the cockpit all around my middle as I looked.

Something about it told me this was an amateur job. Someone had made it by hand. Beside it was a sign that said, "This year's entry from Detroit in the National Soap Box Derby in Akron, Ohio." Taped to the window all around it in a ring were pictures of boys in other racing cars, all homemade. Each picture bore the name of the boy and the year in which he had been Detroit's entry in the Soap Box Derby.

My heart swelled as I looked at those boys in the

cars they had made. In the top picture was this year's winner from Detroit. He was sitting in the very car that stood here now.

That might have been me, I thought. I could learn to make a racer like that if I had rules to follow; I knew it. *I knew that I could.*

I bent close to the window and looked at the smiling freckled face in the picture. I imagined that the words underneath read, "Michael Williams, twelve-year-old winner of this year's race." (Michael, see, not Mike!)

At this point the dream exploded and I walked on slowly. If I could build a good car and run it in a race, that would really show those guys at school! And Patrick wouldn't ever again have to be ashamed of being my twin.

In the next block I found a wonderful junkyard, even better than the one outside Manton near Smitty's Garage. Old rusty engine blocks lay among tall burdock plants. Connecting rods were greasy black with oil. Carburetors and speedometer cases of pot metal had turned white in spots from being rained on.

I turned over a flywheel with a stripped ring gear and studied how the gear had broken. There were so many good old things here I could hardly see them all fast enough. I picked up some scored brake drums and threw them down to grab a gearshift handle. This would make a good brake lever for my coaster. And here were some fancy steering wheels on steering columns, with plastic rims and wire spokes. I picked up one with a yellow rim and held it in my hands, turning it a little, saying quietly, "Bzz-zzz-zzmmm."

Something made me look out into the street, where a big cream-colored car was going past slowly, and I recognized Jim Hoyt's mother. She drove for a half block, then stopped with a loud screech of brakes and backed up. It made me mad that she should treat her brakes like that.

"Michael Williams, is that you?" she called.

I sure felt miserable now. "Yes'm." I walked slowly to the car.

"Hop in, child, I'm going right home."

As the car purred along the street, she asked, "Weren't you in school this afternoon?"

I shrugged and said, "No." I swallowed twice, looked gloomily out of the window, and added, "I don't like school here."

"*Well*," exploded Mrs. Hoyt. "What's that got to do with going?"

I didn't have any answer, so I just didn't say another word.

The Truant Officer

The afternoon paper had already been thrown against the front porch, so I knew that it must be late. I carried it upstairs, feeling tired all over, and spread it on the floor to read what Pogo was saying to Uncle Albert. But I was really wondering what Dad would say when he heard that I had been playing hookey. I could just about make Dad's speech myself:

"Look here, son, do you know the kind of boys who play hookey? They're not our kind, I can tell you. They're boys who will never amount to much. Why can't you be like Patrick? Just once try to make us proud of you, Mike, and quit fooling around. Your mother and I . . ."

Right there I stopped thinking what Dad would say. It hurt too much knowing he would say Mom was ashamed of me. I went to look out the window at the ball game in the lot next door.

There was a storm in the air. Sharp little breezes were rattling the weedy leaves on the tree of heaven by the garage. The sky looked like a dark, heavy wool blanket, and the boys played ball in a queer greenish light. They didn't stop when the thunder started. It made a noise like big bowling balls in an alley a long way off. Patrick laughed and pointed up at a fork of lightning shooting down through the dark, fast and dangerous-looking like a snake's tongue.

Suddenly without any warning hailstones began striking. Putting their arms over their heads, the kids ran for home in all directions. Men who had left their cars at the curbs dashed out and drove into their garages. Up and down the street, women banged windows shut. Hailstones as big as baseballs cracked on the sidewalks, and I saw one break a rusty window screen across the street at the Winslows'.

It all lasted only a few minutes. Then bright yellow streaks of sunlight pointed down through the gray. On our lawn a patch of sunshine lay like a spotlight, with hailstones scattered over the velvety green.

The last of the thunder rolled away somewhere in the direction of the river. When I threw up the kitchen window the air smelled of grass. Kids ran out from the shelter of porches and gathered the hailstones, flinging them at each other.

After supper Dad got out his pipe, and sitting tilted back in his chair, began to puff hard and to look sternly at me. Mom took Patrick and Betsy down to the Hoyts', where they were going to plan a neighborhood Halloween party.

"Mike," Dad said, "Mrs. Hoyt tells me you were over

in a junkyard on Livernois instead of in school this afternoon."

Everything I had stored up inside me all week came out now in a rush—how Patrick had been made a Deputy Boy right away, how Miss Goodfellow had made fun of me, how I had got lost in the hall and run out to the trees where I felt at home, how the other boys had laughed at me when I tried to bat a ball.

"They called me S-screwball," I shouted. "I couldn't stand it."

Dad's pipe had gone out. It took three matches to get it lit again. "If I'd been you, I would have fought them, fought till I dropped."

"I did. Trouble is—I dropped too soon."

"And then you ran away."

"Yes."

Dad sighed. "Well, Mike, your mother and I have talked this over and we're going to let the truant officer decide what to do about it."

"The truant officer?" I would have preferred a spanking. Now, I would have to wait until Monday to learn what punishment was going to happen to me.

Then came the scolding. I hated this worst of all. "I must say," Dad went on, looking hard at a corner of the ceiling, "I'm disappointed in the way you've started out here. Moving to a new place wasn't easy for any of us."

"I'm sure sorry, Dad."

"I *can't* see why you don't try to mingle with the other boys the way Patrick does."

It was so quiet you could have heard the old farm clock tick, but here in Detroit we had only a small electric clock on the stove. So there was no sound at all.

Then I said, "I wanted to mingle, Dad, but they kind of scare me. I'm never sure they'll like me."

"But, good heavens, why not?"

"Well . . . I don't know."

I guess he was thinking (as I was) about the way I walked and couldn't throw straight. Why, I couldn't even pick up a pencil without dropping it half the time.

You can tell when a parent has stopped being mad and begun to be sorry. And that's the worst of all. I got up quick and went to my room to keep from starting to cry. I read *Huckleberry Finn* till I heard the others come home, all laughing and running quick up the back steps from the Hoyts'.

On Monday morning Miss Goodfellow looked at me as cold as icicles and said, "You must report to the Principal's office and tell him why you tried last week to get your education in a junkyard."

Snickers ran all around the classroom, and I saw that Patrick had his head down and was picking at one thumb. Outside, men with a concrete mixer were repairing a break in the sidewalk. I could barely hear the noise of the motor, "Ka-*put*tick, ka-*put*tick," but as I waited in the Principal's outer office it seemed to me my heart was making the same sound: ka-*put*tick, ka-*put*tick, ka-*put*tick.

A buzzer sounded and a girl said, "Mr. Beecham will see you now."

I went into a room where an old bald man sat behind a very large desk. The man's head kept shaking slightly all the time as though he were saying, "No, no, no." The heavy-lidded eyes were like the eyes of a turtle I had seen once by the Manistee River. I couldn't keep from staring at a large dark mole on Mr. Beecham's forehead.

He talked in a whispery voice that was like something in a bad dream. "I have here your attendance record to date, mostly blanks. It has been reported to me that you spent school hours in empty lots last week. Is this true?"

"Y-yes, sir."

"Can you tell me why you were not in your classes?"

I twisted my hands and said the worst thing I could possibly have come out with: "I wasn't happy."

"*Happy?*" His head shook harder than before. His voice shook now too. "Are we supposed to entertain you here, give you candy and movies? *I* used to walk five miles to school through snowdrifts after I had chopped enough wood to keep a farmhouse warm all day. What you need, young man, is a good horsewhipping." He took out a big handkerchief to wipe away little bubbles at the corners of his mouth.

I had to answer, even though I could feel the trembles all over my body. "But—but you were happy because you felt important, and you knew the other boys respected you. That's the way it was for me in Manton. But not here." I hated myself when my lower lip trembled. I bit down hard to stop it.

"Well, I've got no time for boys who don't like the

way we do things." Mr. Beecham handed me a sheet of paper without looking up. "Go down to Room 108 and see what the truant officer says."

I was in the hall alone now. At one end I could see the outside door that might still lead to freedom. I could almost feel the green, and the quiet sense of growing plants in the shelter of the empty lot. Maybe the fort I had made last week would still be standing. For a few seconds I was tempted.

Then I straightened up to make myself as tall as possible and went into Room 108. I knew by now that Mr. Duffy, our gym teacher and also the truant officer, was the idol of the other boys. But how would he treat a boy who preferred junkyards to ball games?

Mr. Duffy sat at a little table in front of some shelves stuffed with papers in folders. As usual he was wearing a sweat shirt with the words, Pontchartrain School, across his chest. "Well, Mike, sit down." His blue eyes glinted like sun on water. He glanced at my attendance record when I handed it to him. "Suppose you tell me what's wrong."

I made fists and drove them together several times, hitting the knuckles hard. Then I told him, "There's not enough to do in the city unless you play ball, and no room to do it in. At home I could ride our horse Nellie, and go camping with Butch, and fish, and wander all over—all over, for miles and miles. It seemed as if everything was mine, as far as I could see.

"Our house had acres of rooms, all with ceilings about a mile high. There was one room full of books, and it

even smelled like books. And the kitchen—why, you could roller-skate in the kitchen. Here we live in a skimpy little flat, and Jimmie Hoyt lives below us. There's no place to keep junk except on a workbench behind the furnace."

"Junk? You like junk?"

"Yes, I do. On the farm we used to have a tool shed so full of junk you couldn't close the door. Here people seem to think you're crazy if you like to go to junkyards. Mrs. Hoyt told my folks I was 'loitering' in one. My mother can fool around secondhand stores all day and no one ever says she's 'loitering.'"

"What do you do with the junk you find?"

"Oh-h, I guess you might call it tinkering. Dad says I 'fool around.' But I can really make things good, Mr. Duffy. I'll show you my coaster some day; I made that years ago. I could do better now, of course." It felt good to boast for a second.

"Last Friday when I was . . . playing hookey" (I grinned at him a little and he grinned too) "I saw a racing car that some boy entered in the Soap Box Derby in Detroit last year—and he won. I thought, Now, that's something I could do."

Mr. Duffy didn't talk while he was doodling on a pad. It looked to me like he was making little cars all over the page. Then he said, "You'd have to follow rules if you entered the Derby. They're very strict about meeting safety regulations, not getting help from adults, and so on. You didn't follow rules very well last week, just did as you pleased."

"Yeah, I goofed all right."

He turned around to the shelves behind him and took down some folders. "Look here, Mike," he said, "these are records of boys who got into trouble—all boys from this school. They don't make us very proud, I can tell you."

I gulped. "Wh-what kind of trouble?"

"Here's one boy who began skipping school and wandering around the streets. Met a man who persuaded him to steal hub caps from parked cars. After a while that got too tame so he watched till a man left his keys in a car and ran in a store to buy something.

The boy was picked up for stealing the car, and now he picks tomatoes for ninety days on the State Farm."

"B-but, Mr. Duffy," I stuttered, "I wouldn't s-steal."

"He wouldn't have either before that man talked him into it."

"City slicker," I said.

"What?"

"My grandma at Manton told me to watch out for city slickers."

"Well, she's right. And here's another boy. They're from nice families, Mike, not bums. This boy got into a street gang that met at night in an empty lot. To be initiated he had to steal a ring from a store. So he went to a dime store and took one and didn't get caught. But the whole gang began stealing bicycles, sold some to a bicycle-riding concession in one of the parks. The man suspected them and traced the number of a license they had overlooked. Bang! All eight of them are doing time on the State Farm now."

"Golly!" I had never dreamed of getting into real trouble like that.

"We get a lot of stories like this, Mike." He put the folders back on the shelf and opened a brand-new one. And there at the top of the page I saw my name, "Williams, Michael."

"Oh, gee, do you keep a file on *me?*"

He looked really sad. Now I could see why all the boys liked him. It was because he liked the boys, and I could see he liked me too.

"I'll have to, Mike, all year. It's a rule about truancy.

I have to follow rules too. Well, let's see if we can keep this record sheet clean except for eight words."

"Eight words?"

"On the first of each month from now on—October through May—you'll report to me. If you have a record of no truancy trouble, I'll write in 'negative.' Then at the end of the school year, we'll . . . we'll tear it up, shall we?"

"And burn it?" I asked hopefully.

He smiled. "Okay. And burn it." Suddenly his tone was very serious. "Patrick is your twin, isn't he?"

"Yeah." I dropped my eyes. Right away I felt awful again.

"He give you a bad time?"

I had to shake my head. "He's kind of nice to me usually," I admitted. "Makes it worse than if he hated me. He acts ashamed when I do something wrong, like I was a shadow that didn't follow him right."

Mr. Duffy stood up and grabbed my hand between his and squeezed it hard. "You don't have to be anyone's shadow, Mike," he said. "You go it at your own pace, and I'll stand behind you—as long as you keep your record clean. But if you don't, I'm afraid it will make me mad."

"Okay, thanks, Mr. Duffy."

"And, Mike, let me tell you some good news now. If you like to tinker, Detroit's the very place to live. You can visit car factories, foundries, midget auto races, even junkyards."

"But no garage like Smitty's in Manton, I'll bet, with a guy in charge who knows all about motors."

"I dare say you'll even find good auto mechanics in Detroit," said Mr. Duffy. "Like your father, for instance." He picked up my attendance sheet. "Now about this hookey . . ."

I looked out at white clouds drifting high in the blue morning sky. "I won't play hookey any more," I said. "I got tired of not knowing where to go. It's terribly lonesome, you know. It was just . . . those boys . . . the others called me 'Screwball.' "

"I heard about that. Some of us talked it over one day after gym, Mike. I told them you'd been crippled by polio. It's on your health record, you know."

I clasped my hands hard between my knees. "Why did you have to tell 'em that?" I asked.

"Things are easier to face if you admit them," said Mr. Duffy. "Now remember, report to me on the first of October. You'll have to make up the work you missed. But also, Michael, collect all the junk you want. Tinker all you please."

A bell rang. "If you hurry, you can get back to your room before the last bell."

"Yes, sir." Well, that hadn't been bad, after all. I could sure see why the other fellows liked Mr. Duffy.

The Tree House

I don't know if you've ever been around chickens any. If you have, you've probably seen a half-grown chick take a lot of trouble struggling through a very small hole to get out of the chicken yard. Maybe it wants some grass on the outside that looks better than the food it's getting. Maybe it spots a shiny bug.

Anyway, it gets out. And then runs half crazy up and down along the fence, trying to get back in. It's too dumb, I guess, to see the hole it got out through; or if it does see it, it doesn't know what that hole was ever used for.

It keeps running. It looks through the mesh, and the other chickens seem to be in a real chicken heaven, full of food scraps and fights and dust between their toes. They don't pay any attention to the chicken on the outside. They don't say, "Over here, fellow, come through here." No, they just go on eating and scratching and learning to cluck.

Well, there I was.

Mr. Duffy had welcomed me back to the school, and he was just as nice to me in gym as he was to the others—not any nicer, because he's not like that. But Miss Goodfellow went right ahead being real mean to me. Even Mr. Whitman in our social studies class made sarcastic remarks. That's one thing I can't stand, sarcasm. Like this: "I'm sure Mike wants to tell us some of the products of Detroit—something besides junk, that is. Rise and shine, Michael."

He was never sarcastic to Patrick. Everyone always accepted Patrick for what he was, a nice, good boy who didn't make bad mistakes, yet never managed to act too good either. He just simply knew how to stay in the groove. Parents and teachers smiled at him, while kids his age acted as if he had always been their leader, no questions asked.

Kids didn't really seem to dislike me; they just made like I wasn't there. It's worse being ignored, I guess, than being yelled at and scolded.

They didn't ask me to play ball any more, even though I had made up my mind I'd learn if it killed me. So now I didn't have to. But they didn't ask me to do other things either.

Of course, there was no point in my joining the Little League. But when they all went swimming at the Y pool on a Saturday they didn't ask me to go along. So Patrick had to tell them that I was a good swimmer.

Well, after Patrick told them I did go with the others. But somehow they never asked me to take part in any of the races, and when they played water polo with a big ball no one ever threw it my way. I swam around, but you feel mighty lonely in a pool full of boys if they never look in your direction.

Of course, both Patrick and I joined the Boy Scouts. Mr. Duffy was the leader for our age group that year, and he came to see our folks the second week. There was never any doubt about a boy's being taken into the Scouts if he wanted to belong. But no one could make the other guys really welcome me.

We'd take up some project like tying knots and mounting them on a board. I never could see why so many Boy Scouts tied so many knots, but it wasn't bad learning. While we were working, the other kids talked to each other and all around me but not often right to me. If they did, it would be like they were looking down from someplace. This made me sore because I'm not dumb. My knots were as good as any done by the other guys.

I guess I looked puny working away at them, and that must have made the other kids uncomfortable. Maybe with girls it's just the opposite; maybe they like the littlest, puniest girls. I wouldn't know.

And when we had cocoa and cookies or popcorn, I always seemed to get stuck next to Mr. Duffy, like the chicken the others don't bother to peck at. Maybe I just imagined that I was ignored, but it sure felt real to me.

Then for a while I didn't care too much how the guys treated me because we got a car—our family, I mean. While we did our homework Dad and Mom talked forever about down payments and high prices.

One Saturday Dad said, "Found a used-car lot over on Livernois that's supposed to have some good buys. Come along, Mike." Yes, he asked me, not Patrick, to go with him. And why not? We all knew I had more know-how about car engines than my twin ever would.

I felt good riding in the pickup beside Dad. This was the same street where I had played hookey, but nothing seemed the same now. Instead of frowning down on me, the stores and people smiled. I was not surprised when Dad turned in at the very lot where I had been caught by the owner looking at his used cars and had got scared and run on down the street.

The same man I had seen there before came out of a shed. After one quick glance at me he winked. "Well, well, brought your father this time, eh, Sonny? What can I show you, Mister?"

"I don't know what you have." Dad preferred to do his own looking.

"Take a look around the lot." The man waved his cigar in the air. "If you see something you want, I'll be in the office."

We went past all the shiny, nearly new, expensive models to the rows farther back in the lot. It didn't take Dad long to make a choice, a ten-year-old black four-door with a standard shift, a heater, a radio—and a price tag close to his budget.

The salesman was there before we could hunt for him.

"Here's the keys. Try it."

It started the instant Dad turned the key hard over. He gunned it gently to warm it up and slowly started over the gravel onto Livernois. Compared to the old pickup, it had a silky clutch and velvet brakes. And it steered as though it and Dad had been made to go together, he said.

"Let's take it, Mike," said Dad.

I tried to get rid of a lump in my throat. Why did I want to cry? I wonder. I was sure excited.

The man put a SOLD sign on the windshield.

"We'll come back next Saturday to make a payment on it," said Dad.

When we went to get our "new" car Patrick was up the street playing kick-the-can with a big gang. But can you *imagine* not wanting to go pick up our car with the rest of us? Mom and Betsy insisted on coming, and at the last minute Charlotte yelled, "Me, too. I'm coming."

"Women," Dad said, smiling at me.

For a moment when I saw the car with the SOLD sign on it I had a shock of disappointment. I had been dreaming of the car all week. Now I wondered what Charlotte must think of this old thing—Charlotte, whose family had one of the newest, biggest, shiniest cars on the block.

Then I ran forward and put my hand on the hood and joy ran right through me, hot and fast. This was our very own, the Williams family car. So what if it wasn't new? I loved it.

While Dad was inside the bright office with the salesman, I slid behind the steering wheel and gripped the rim. It was wavy underneath with finger-sized ripples.

"Bzz-zzm, bz-zzzummmm," I said, and dreamed I drove a racer.

In Detroit a car is more important than a home. Not to have a car in a big city is almost like not having feet. I was only sorry the motor of the "new" car was in good condition and did not need tinkering.

Dad had to take us all sightseeing the first Saturday after we had our own car. "I always wanted to drive my family to the city," he said. "All the time we lived on the farm I kept remembering Detroit."

I wanted to like Detroit for Dad's sake, but I'd have given about anything if we'd turned around and headed up the highway toward Manton. Instead, we drove to huge buildings at Grand Boulevard and Second Street, and Dad showed us where the auto industry offices are. Inside the arcade in the Fisher Building sleek gray marble walls reach up to arches way above your head.

"Pretty," said Mom and Betsy, gazing up.

"Can we go to the movies?" asked Patrick.

We went through the concourse under the buildings to eat in a cafeteria. Here men had tunneled long avenues underground like gophers. I realized how important this city was, but I wondered if I would ever feel I belonged here. In the cafeteria Pat ordered twice as much as me and got scolded for costing so much.

Downtown around the river were more tall buildings shooting up to scrape the sky. Dad took us in an elevator to the top of one; I think it must have been about thirty stories high. We looked out and down at the river, where puffs of steam were like little white flowers.

"Look how far you can see," said Mom admiringly.

"Let's go home," Pat insisted. "I want to play ball before dark."

The next Saturday when we took a picnic to a place called Belle Isle, Patrick wouldn't even go.

"Mrs. Hoyt asked me to lunch," he said. "You don't care, do you, Mom? Mike can go with you."

Yes, I thought bitterly, I'd have to, because Mrs. Hoyt hadn't invited me—just the Three Musketeers: Hubert and Patrick and of course her son Jimmie.

But anyway we took Charlotte along this time, so that made it more fun. Mr. Whitman had told us in social studies that Belle Isle had been used for a prison for Southern soldiers in the Civil War. But now it's full of black squirrels and picnickers and peacocks.

Very small black French ponies hitched to carts take people for rides. Kind of fun for Betsy and Charlotte. Boys don't go for pony carts.

What I really liked was the little train at the Royal Oak Zoo, where we went after we'd eaten our picnic lunch. It was a perfect small-scale model of a real locomotive with an important little whistle that made me laugh out loud. I could have ridden on that till dark, but of course the girls had to see the monkeys— and snakes, of all things!

But after we got home the day was spoiled for me when I discovered Patrick and Hubert and Jimmie had got at my workbench and messed it up. They'd got bored playing ball, or run out of men to take the bases.

Then they'd gone down in the basement to fool around.

I went down while Mom was getting supper, because that week I'd found an old blowtorch on a junk heap and I wondered if Dad would let me use it for something, and if so, what. Anyway, I wanted to look at it again.

The place was a *mess*. I'm not too neat myself, but about tools I'm pretty fussy. One of the guys had apparently sawed some fresh tree limbs somewhere and left the saw lying on the floor, with damp greenish sawdust in its teeth. They'd emptied my coffee can of nails and mixed them with a tin of bolts. My blowtorch was over in one corner, and an old bellows I'd found not long ago had been ripped so it was no good any more.

I went yelling up the back outside stairs for Dad to come down and see. Dad was tired from all the driving, so instead of figuring out a fair explanation and punishment like he usually did, he gave Patrick a couple of terrific slaps and said, "You get your pals down here and put everything back the way you found it. Hop to it. No supper till it's okay."

Patrick gave me a look I won't forget in a hurry, and I went out quickly to follow Dad upstairs. I wished I hadn't told on Patrick. I wished Dad didn't somehow act as if he was protecting a weak little bird when he talked about me. I thought I would never live it down.

Luckily for me on Monday something more important had the kids all upset. When we came home from school, we saw a power shovel in the middle of the baseball diamond next door. It was eating away at the dirt like a great big dinosaur. I watched the man at the controls guide the dipper down to gobble bites of sand with an icing of weeds and burs. Three dipper-fuls filled a truck, which went away down the alley with the dirt while another truck took its place.

We had known that the lot was for sale. The boys always hung their coats over the FOR SALE sign before they went up to bat. But somehow no one had ever thought it would really be sold. I wasn't as mad as the other kids. In fact I have to admit I was a little bit glad they wouldn't be playing baseball so close to our house, where I had to see Patrick being a hero every afternoon.

The kids moved on up the street to another empty lot just this side of our school, and the games went right on where they had left off. But after supper they took to jumping down into the big square hole that had been dug for a basement. And on Saturday we sat around under the wild cherry tree and watched the men set the concrete blocks and then cement them to-gether with mortar to make the basement walls.

One morning they began laying the flooring and I was so interested I was almost late for school. I was surprised at the way the foundation boards were laid edgewise right on top of the concrete basement walls. Then squares for the rooms were marked off with more boards, and big joists laid edgewise in each room square and nailed into place. The frame was just laid on top of the concrete!

Why, I thought, the whole house could be blown off and whirled to the Land of Oz. I hope they know what they're doing. Later Dad explained the force of gravity to me.

The other kids didn't care how the house was made—except Jim Hoyt, who often hung around with me mornings and noons to watch the men working. Jimmie sort of liked to know how things were made, same as me.

The subflooring was laid down diagonally, starting at a corner and going right across the whole floor area. "That makes a triangle," said a workman, grinning to see that Jim and I were interested. "Every single board of the subflooring makes a triangle with two sides of the house. Then the hardwood floor goes on top. The diagonals are for strength and rigidity."

"Yeah." Jim threw away his apple core, and as we started toward school he said, "You know, there's a big, big oak tree at the back of the lot where we're playing baseball now. We could make a tree house there. You know the one that sorta opens out its branches above the lowest limb crotch."

Say, now, that was an idea! But the next second after I'd said, "Great," I realized it would be right behind the baseball diamond and I wouldn't be very welcome there.

All the same, I couldn't keep away from the thought. The other guys went for it too. And when the next Saturday came I was down at the lot early, with Patrick, ready to go to work.

"The first thing," said Jimmie, "is to have plenty of boards. Where'll we get 'em?"

"Buy a few," suggested Larry Winslow, whose Dad had money for everything.

Richard Depew shook his head. "That's okay for

you, Larry, but the rest of us have used up our allowances on our Little League uniforms."

They all looked at me—I hadn't bought one. Why should I? It made me mad, to see what they expected. Right when I had a chance to stand in good with the guys again, I thought, Why should *I* furnish the boards for their old tree house?

I said, "I'm saving my allowance to buy supplies for a racer."

"A what?"

"I'm gonna build a racer for the Soap Box Derby next year."

"Wanna bet?"

"That's way next summer."

"It doesn't matter," Patrick was defending me again. "There must be some better way to get boards than just buying them." He made me mad sometimes, sticking up for me, just as I felt I had the courage to stick up for myself!

"Everybody ask his own dad," suggested Hubert reasonably. When Patrick said something the kids accepted it, so there was no more pressure on me to buy the boards.

Well, believe it or not, our dads thought it was a good idea for us to have a tree house. It would save wear and tear on everyone's flat, for one thing (and give us a chance to work off steam, according to Mr. McMurtrie). So we really built a dandy.

Jim explained how the workmen made floors in the new house, and he and I got the job of laying the floor. It was almost level, too, when we finished. Patrick

nailed slats up the side of the tree for a ladder, and
Larry and Hubert put the walls in place. We didn't
plan a window—too complicated.

We just walled in three sides, and then Jimmie
brought down a curtain to close off the fourth. Jim's
father works for an automobile upholstery company and
always has big samples of materials left at the end
of the year. This curtain was good and heavy, something
he called rep; and it was a beautiful bright red. Patrick,
being the tallest, got the job of nailing it to a lintel
that went between two walls. When it was finished, the
hut was about four and a half by six feet, which is
pretty crowded for six boys but pretty big for a city
oak tree.

"There won't be more than two or three up here at
once, anyway," reasoned Richard.

So there we were, as snug as bugs. Or I should say,
there they were. It was our tree house, all of us. The
parents knew it, but the boys sort of forgot.

They were polite to me when I came up the lath
ladder and lifted the curtain to scrounge my way in
over the sill. They just said, "Oh, it's Mike," and sounded
surprised. Sometimes I thought they stopped talking
the minute my head came up over the edge of the floor.

I know fellows can imagine these things. And could
be I was extra sensitive because everyone knew I was
on the truant officer's probation list. They'd all know it
when the first of next month came and I reported to
him again. I was sure of that.

I tell you, once you get outside the fence that sets
off the rules of the chicken yard you sure do forget how

to get back in. After a while I never came down to the tree house when the baseball games were going on, but just after supper or early in the morning. It was really most fun when I was there all alone.

Then one afternoon right before supper I stuck my head in under the curtain and smelled smoke. Worse than that, I saw Patrick stub out a cigarette real fast. Hubert grabbed up an old fruit-jar lid full of cigarette stubs and ashes and pushed it behind Jimmie, next to him.

I decided that was why they sometimes stopped talking when I went into our tree house. But this could lead to real trouble. And I didn't want another Williams twin on probation!

I didn't know what to do, so I took the coward's way. I pretended I hadn't noticed anything wrong.

"Hi, Patrick," I said, "Mom wants you to come to supper. We've got to eat early. It's a P.T.A. night."

"Okay, Mike, I'll be along right away." I knew when I wasn't wanted, so I let the curtain fall and climbed back down the lath ladder.

As I walked through the wooded part of the lot, scuffing the dead leaves, I wondered what a good, strong, red-blooded Rover Boy would have done in my place. I should probably have pointed out that they were doing a wrong as well as dangerous thing. But who was I to find fault with others? Anyway, I hadn't, and now it was too late.

From that time on I began to feel that Patrick was really turning against me.

Mr. Duffy Takes Us Sailing

He began to avoid me even when we went to bed. We shared the same back bedroom, overlooking the garage, and at bedtime we had always horsed around a little bit together, kidded about girls, and fussed about who brushed his teeth and used the bathroom first. Patrick even liked me to read to him sometimes after he was in his pajamas and lying with his arms above his head, "easing off," as he called it.

Now he waited till I was in bed with the light off before he quit studying, or pretending to study. He already had the habit of leaving for school every day before me because of his Deputy Boy duty, and after school too we had never had much companionship. But now there was a difference even at the table. If I made a little too much noise with my soup, I'd look up and find him staring at me like a regular devil.

He never talked to me about the cigarettes, or for

that matter, anything else any more. He must have wondered if I had told on him and the other boys. But he'd have died, I guess, rather than ask. Except when he looked hard and angry about something I did wrong, it was as if I wasn't there. From other boys that's bad; from your own twin it's awful. You have to feel you're there. You have to know you exist. I began to wonder, not what I was and who, but *why* too. It was a terrible time.

Finally Mr. Duffy noticed, in gym class one day. We were playing basketball and I'd tried to guard Patrick from getting down to make a basket.

I'd been fanning my arms fast the way a guard does, and Patrick kept bouncing the ball to one side and then the other. He kept inching ahead, and of course I was running backward, doing the best I could to keep him from shooting clear to someone else. Then he bounced the ball right at me and pushed me over to the floor.

It was a foul, and Mr. Duffy blew his whistle hard. When he took the ball from Patrick, he said, "What's the big idea, Williams, you trying to kill your brother?"

Patrick didn't look at me, but said as if he were talking about cats (which he hates), "Can I help it if he can't keep his feet?"

Mr. Duffy didn't say any more, just blew his whistle again while he threw the ball up between us. Patrick knocked it clean away from me to Hubert, who bounced it fast down to their end and made a basket easy as pie. Their side cheered, and that was that.

But when we were dismissed to go to our lockers Mr. Duffy put his hand on my arm and said, so low the other fellows didn't hear, "Can I see you at my desk when you're dressed?"

"Sure." Even if I hadn't wanted to go, I had to mind the truant officer—from now on. Sometimes it made me nervous, even though he was so nice and the scout-master and all.

The other boys from our tree-house gang all went off together. The four big ones—Hubert and Patrick, Jimmie and Richard Depew, all Deputy Boys—had to be at the corners to get the little kids safely across the street. And Larry Winslow always tagged along wherever Richard went, just the way Dickie Fells followed me around.

Mr. Duffy was waiting for me at his desk. He had showered and looked clean and rosy in his white sweat shirt, but his bright kind blue eyes were sad.

"What's wrong now, Mike?" he asked.

I wished I could tell him; I sure did. But then it would be worse than ever with the other fellows. What good would it do to tell on them?

"Nothing," I said, looking down, knowing too late that it sounded sulky. But I couldn't help that.

"The rest of the boys still give you a bad time, don't they?"

"You know, Mr. Duffy, when there's a weaker chicken in the yard the others always go for it. And if it's got any blood on it, good night!"

He laughed, then sobered real fast. He fidgeted with some papers on his desk, and said like he was trying to get the truth out of me, "But there *is* something wrong."

I thought about the cigarettes and how those boys would have a right to hate me if I tattled. So I looked down at the floor some more and said, "It's nothing really, Mr. Duffy. They just pick on me. If you tell 'em not to, they'll think I've been whining. And I—I don't like to be—protected."

He didn't say anything for such a long while I was afraid I had hurt his feelings. Then he said, "No, of course not. Well, we'll think of something. So long, Mike."

He thought of something all right—something perfectly wonderful. On Tuesday evening we had a Boy Scout meeting down in the Baptist Church basement. First we made a report on how much we had collected for UNICEF on Halloween night.

In Detroit on Halloween you go out dressed up in costumes to beg from door to door. But instead of yelling, "Trick or treat," you call out, "Help the poor." It works just the same, though. Some of us had had cream cartons with slots cut in the little pouring spouts and had collected coins to send to the United Nations International Children's Emergency Fund.

Mr. Duffy was proud of our troop. On our street in a couple of blocks we had collected over nineteen dollars. People like Larry Winslow's father really like kids and had stuffed fifty-cent pieces into our cartons.

After our report and some study about how to help repair wiring in our homes, we had our cocoa. Mrs. Duffy had sent fresh cookies and marshmallows to melt in the cocoa. So we all felt good, but in a minute we felt even better.

"I've been wondering," said Mr. Duffy, "if you boys might like to go in for some water sports. I've got a little sailboat at the Bay View Club. I take it out about every Saturday. Do you think you might like to learn to sail? Maybe if you take to it, you might end up being Sea Scouts. There's lots of sailing in the river and on Lake St. Clair."

Gee, we gasped; and then all the fellows talked at once:

"That sounds keen."—"When could we go?"—"How many?"

Mr. Duffy was doodling on his Boy Scout manual. The pictures he drew looked like little triangles. Then I made out they were sailboats. "I thought of dividing up my troop into two groups," he said, putting some wavy lines among the triangles for water. "You six from your street next Saturday, and the other five the week after. We have to go while this good autumn weather lasts.

"Suppose you talk it over with your parents and let me know tomorrow in gym class."

"Yes, sir."—"Oh, sure, Mr. Duffy. *Which* Saturday did you say? This one?" Everyone was so excited and yelling so loud I thought they'd have the police down there.

Patrick even looked over at me and grinned. He has a nice white smile; I guess it pays to brush your teeth.

It took some persuading of our mothers, and a lot of telephoning back and forth and a special call to Mrs. Duffy before they'd let us go that Saturday. Somehow Mom had the idea that sailing on Lake St. Clair might be dangerous. Even when Dad said he'd heard it was very shallow, she still had to be talked around. And so did Mrs. Hoyt, who seemed to think that because Jim was so heavy (practically fat) he might sink.

We could all swim, and our dads pooh-poohed the worrying and said of course we could go. And Mrs. Duffy said over the phone, "Do you think Andrew would take your boys if there were any danger?" She sounded quite huffy.

The rest of the week dragged for us all. The night before our trip the sky looked wet and cloudy, but the weathermen promised a clear Saturday. And they were right.

On Saturday we were up hours before it grew light. I love the early morning. Grandma used to say, "The morning hour has gold in its mouth." I don't know what she meant, but there's something magic about the first morning hours. In the city I could feel it now the way I used to in the country. The dark and cool of night had some special delight that people lost in the bright glare of day.

Mr. Duffy picked us up in his station wagon and stowed our food baskets in back with his. Then away we went. Light came up gradually behind the big old-fashioned houses along Grand Boulevard. Among the fine old homes were islands of factories and railroad tracks.

"The city grows too fast," said Mr. Duffy.

As he turned out Jefferson Avenue he gave us advice about sailing. "We tack up the river to where it widens out into Lake St. Clair," he said. "That means we let the wind drive our sails in a diagonal course to the opposite shore. When we get almost there, I yell, 'Stand by to come about.' That means duck down flat unless you want your heads to come off. Then I swing the boom over to catch the wind from the other direction. That drives us back diagonally to this side again. The third time we make it into the lake.

"Don't lean too far out at any time. And no matter what happens, don't be scared. You're safe with me." He sounded as happy as a little kid.

We drove out a cindered path to the low green-and-white cottage of the Bay View Club. Sky and river everywhere were coral pink.

When I first saw the sailboat I was pretty disappointed. It was just one of many, with a mast rising like a young tree in a grove. The name *Dulcie Mae* was painted on one end, and I thought it was a pretty silly name.

"All aboard," called Mr. Duffy gaily. "First we make shipshape." He helped us one by one down into the little boat that rocked teasingly under our uncertain steps. Once aboard we scrambled over her solid deck and stowed our food in a tiny space called a galley.

To get out of the well Patrick helped Mr. Duffy pull the boat slowly into the channel, hand over hand on the mooring lines.

Mr. Duffy gave a final shove at a pile with the spinnaker pole and hoisted the jib. The breeze caught the *Dulcie Mae's* nose and straightened her into the current. Mr. Duffy unfurled the mainsail with long pulls on the halyard. (See how easy it is to pick up these terms? He told us what he was doing, and I think I remember it right.)

Now we were on our way! The wind caught my breath and stung my eyes. There was not a sound except the lap of little waves under the bow and the steady *slish* of the bow-wave.

The green scallops of the shore were soon far away. Mr. Duffy gave us orders and we did exactly as he said, no argument. He let Hubert steer on the first tack, Patrick on the next, and Jimmie on the one that took us out into Lake St. Clair.

Each time he shouted, "Stand by to come about," we all ducked as flat as possible so that when the boom swung over the cockpit no one got bumped.

"Good lads," said Mr. Duffy.

We met the big ore and grain boats that use this channel on their way from Lake Superior, and passed boats going in the opposite direction, from Detroit to Chicago, with decks full of cars. Sometimes one of the crew waved to us.

The channel was marked with nun buoys (with cone-shaped caps) and can buoys (with cylindrical tops). Going up the lake we didn't have to tack. The boat was like a bird flying very fast, skimming the pearly lake.

The channel through Lake St. Clair has been dredged to make it deep enough for the steamers. None of the lake is more than twenty feet deep, and many acres of it are so shallow that grass grows out of the water. Mr. Duffy pointed out the lightship just off the channel.

"It's like a lighthouse," he said, "except that it's more practical in a mud-bottom lake to anchor a ship with lights at her masthead than it is to build a lighthouse."

No one was on the ship. Lighting generators throbbed, and every few seconds a bell tolled. "It's controlled from shore by radio," said Mr. Duffy. It was a ghostly thing.

A blue haze settled over the water, and we seemed to be in the middle of nowhere, with no land in sight.

"It's past noon," said Jim suddenly. "How about lunch?" He was always thinking of food. But I realized I was awfully hungry too. I'd been too excited before to notice.

Mr. Duffy loosened the halyard and dropped the mainsail. He told Larry how to lower the jib and he let me throw in the anchor, which made a loud *plosh* when it hit the water.

Soon hamburgers were hissing and crackling in hot butter on the gasoline stove. The gulls must have smelled them, for they circled around at a safe distance screeching, "Ple-ease! Ple-ease!"

Mr. Duffy put corn on the cob in a fat kettle over the other burner and got ready a pot of coffee for himself. We laid out all the things our mothers had sent—fried chicken and potato salad, a chocolate cake and cookies.

"We won't starve," chuckled Jim.

Food never tasted so good! The corn was so hot that the butter ran right down to my elbows. We saved scraps to throw to the gulls, but some of the chocolate from the cake stayed on our faces.

"No women aboard," Mr. Duffy reminded us, "so you'll have to clean up and wash the dishes." He scraped the garbage into a bowl and threw it into the lake, saying, "Yagaboo!"

"What does that mean?"

"That means, 'Good-by,'" he told us. "The South Sea

Islanders say that, I've been told, when they throw something overboard."

"Yagaboo! Yagaboo!" we yelled.

The gulls said nothing. They were busy gobbling scraps. We were full of food and contentment and sort of sleepy. It was so quiet when the gulls left I could hear my heart beating. Maybe you know something more fun than being out on a boat in a calm quiet place with other fellows, but I don't.

Well, it was fun until Mr. Duffy spoke—and then for me the sun went under a cloud. "We'll start back," he said. "But first, boys, I want to talk to you all about something important." He didn't look at me, but I supposed he was going to defend me to the others. And my pulses began to feel thick as if twice as much blood was trying to get through; and I was hot all over.

"I have heard a rumor that some of my best athletes are smoking," he said in a low voice, that nevertheless carried far over the water.

"Now I'm not accusing any of you, you understand. I'm going to talk to the other scouts next Saturday; and then I'll speak to the whole gym class some day. But some of you boys are leaders in your class—and you can exert either a good or a bad influence. Sometimes it can be argued whether a thing is good or bad. But there's no question that cigarettes at your age are bad."

He told us there was a risk in accepting cigarettes from strangers because they might be doped. (There is something called marijuana that can foul you up and make you very likely to get into real trouble.)

"So where your responsibility starts," said Mr. Duffy,

still in that low, sort of sad voice, "is in refusing the cigarette in the first place. Now you may ask what kind of trouble you could get into. Well, I'll tell you. In our school files we have a number of records of fellows who started stealing little things like candy or cigarettes from a grocery, or maybe just a comic book occasionally. And they ended up doing time at the State Farm.

"Does that sound bad to you? Well, the boys who got in trouble were kids just like you, from nice families and all. But they hadn't learned to say No. So I'm telling you now, say No to the first offer of a cigarette or of anything your folks have already told you is wrong. I don't want any more black marks against our school."

The guys all looked at me, and he added, "Don't go on blaming Mike for playing hookey. He might have got into serious trouble, but he didn't—and now I don't think he will. Well, I guess that's all."

We were sure quiet going back, and I had the feeling none of the kids wanted to work with me. They all thought I'd tattled on them. I didn't know where Mr. Duffy had found out about the cigarettes, but he sure spoiled my day. I don't blame him, you understand, any more than I blame the other fellows for thinking they had a right to be sore at me. It was just one of those things that happen—only why do they keep happening to me?

The sun was setting when we got to the Bay View Club again. The clear orange light of the sky made the grass and trees brilliant green. The river looked

cold and mysterious, rippling with little twisting glints
that reflected lights on shore.

Well, you might have known I would do something
at the last that the other fellows could openly blame
me for.

Mr. Duffy had the four big fellows mooring the boat
alongside the landing, making bow and stern lines fast
to piles, while Larry and I were supposed to be making
shipshape—taking down fly screens and all like that.

And you know what I did? I somehow managed to
fall off that boat and into the water after she was in her
well. Even if I had never done anything wrong before,
that would have finished me for life. Don't ask me how
it happened. It happened, that's all!

I think I was trying to show off because I was nervous about the fellows thinking I'd tattled. I was saying, "Look at me. I'm okay." I was tempting fate.

Anyhow, I teetered along the edge of the boat till I lost my balance and went splash, into the coldest water I'd ever felt. If it could only have happened out in the middle of Lake St. Clair, where there would have been a smidgen of danger! But here, safe back in harbor, I went overboard clear up to my neck.

I was too ashamed to holler for help. Patrick and Jim were staggering up the catwalk when I went over. Patrick said, "Oh, my gosh," in the most disgusted tone.

And Hubert yelled, "Good grief, now what?"

Jim muttered, "Once a screwball always a screwball!"

Poor Mr. Duffy, I felt sorriest of all for him. I felt as if he had planned this day on ship partly to draw us all together, keep me from feeling like a dope. Boy, he didn't know what a job he had!

Patrick jumped right into the water beside me to help me out. He could have waited; the water didn't come over my head where I fell in. But then he wouldn't have seemed like a hero. Oh, I'll admit I'm a little sore about the whole thing.

He fished me out and then we both undressed in the back of the station wagon while the other fellows stored away the baskets and pulled canvas over the galley and did all the things I'd wanted to help with.

"You would have to show off!" muttered Patrick, wrapping himself in a blanket. Lucky that Mr. Duffy always planned for emergencies. "Here, take this lap robe. Get into it."

I didn't say anything because my teeth were chattering, and I was so ashamed that my heart seemed chattering too.

The other kids were as embarrassed as if they had an idiot with them. But Mr. Duffy was nice as ever and drove us home as if nothing out of the way had happened.

When the other guys got out and said their thanks and good-bys I stayed a minute to fold up the lap robe. "Better run in quick, Mike, and get into dry clothes."

"Mr. Duffy, uh—who told you about the cigarettes?"

"Why, one of the girls, Mike. I can't tell you who."

"Well, those guys—Patrick and all—think I told you." I explained about how I'd found them smoking in our tree house.

Mr. Duffy sighed a deep, deep sigh and said, "Guess we're not through the woods yet, Mike. Keep your chin up, boy. You'll live through it."

"Yes, sir, I guess so. Anyway, thanks for a—a wonderful day."

The City Slicker

I don't know how long Patrick had been talking at home about earning some extra money before I noticed it. We avoided each other, so he may have had the idea a long time before I saw the stranger hanging around outside our school. But I connected the two things in my mind, and I suppose now I always will.

(This was long before I saw his card in Patrick's arithmetic book and knew that his name was Harry Bonham.) I'll take it slow, try to remember it just as it happened. I came out of school one afternoon and saw this long, low, expensive car parked down the street a little ways. A man sat at the wheel and the minute I saw him I knew what Grandma had meant when she said, "City slicker."

He had a real thin mouth and thin eyes, all pale, no color at all to speak of, at least from where I saw him across the street. You wouldn't notice eyebrows or hair on a man like that anyway, just the eyes—small, narrow, and mean—and the mouth, also small, narrow, and mean. Later I saw him hanging around the lot where

the kids played ball. Finally I even came to our tree house one afternoon late and found him there, standing on the ground talking to Patrick—my own twin.

But not so fast now!

At first he just parked near the school, watching the kids go home. But one day I was late getting dressed after gym. Dad was always accusing me of dawdling, and that time I was sorry I had dawdled. For when I got to the corner the little kids had all crossed and the Deputy Boys were free to go home. There they stood, talking to this character, this creep, and then they stopped (like it was some big secret) when I went past. I tell you, I felt bad.

At suppertime Patrick said to Dad, "All the guys have bicycles except me."

"Mike hasn't," said Dad.

"Oh, well, Mike!" It was the way he often said my name now.

"Never mind that kind of talk," Dad said sternly.

Patrick started to say, "All I said—"

But Dad answered, "I heard you, young man. You don't have to have a bicycle. I'm just ready to make the last payment on our car and you talk about a bicycle."

"Oh, gee whiz, Dad, everyone else——"

"We're not talking about everyone else, we're talking about the Williamses. In the first place, you don't get any expensive equipment that Mike doesn't have."

"Well," said Patrick, "we could own it together."

"You know good and well who'd get the good of that arrangement," said Mom, though she usually didn't enter into arguments.

Patrick didn't say any more. But next day I saw him with Jim down at the corner drugstore, and that fellow came up in his car and got out and started talking to them again.

That evening Patrick had a new ax to grind. "Why can't I peddle papers, Dad?" he wanted to know as he finished his second helping of pie. "Jim and Hubert are going to ask their dads too. We could do it after school. We won't be able to play ball much longer when it starts to rain and snow."

"Why this sudden urge to earn money?" Dad demanded. "Isn't your allowance enough? We figured you could take a girl to a movie once a week on it and still save a little."

Patrick laughed with Dad. They both knew he was too shy and too young to take a girl to a movie. "No, but I've got ideas for Christmas," he said then. "I want to give nice things to everybody."

"And earn enough to buy a bicycle," said Dad. "I know."

"Well, what's wrong with that if I earn it myself?"

Mom spoke up again, in a soft, firm voice she uses when she disapproves of something but doesn't want to hurt your feelings. "We've never believed in giving big expensive presents at Christmas, Patrick. Something you make yourself is better."

"Yeah, I know. You said you used to make pen wipers and lamp mats," answered Patrick with something like a smile.

"There are still things to make if you have the intelligence and ability," Mom answered tartly. "I'll bet Mike could think of a few."

Matter of fact, I had already begun thinking what I could make for Christmas. But I didn't like the hateful way Patrick looked at me when she said that.

Patrick wasn't the kind of boy who enjoys making things ("fooling around," as Dad put it). Jimmie did, but he was the only one of the Three Musketeers who liked puttering in the basement. Patrick and Hubert wanted something to show for what they did, not just in the future but right away—like a pay check at the end of the month.

There are lots of boys like that, and I guess they

ought to start earning money some way when they're twelve or so. Patrick will probably make a lot more money than I will when we grow up—but I wonder if maybe I won't have more fun.

Now I noticed that Patrick often told Mom he would be at our tree house and then didn't show up there after all. Once I went down to tell him to come to supper and there wasn't a soul around. That's the time I found this man's card in Patrick's arithmetic book, which he'd left on the floor in the tree house.

"Harry Bonham, Publications," it said, with an address on Livernois Avenue. I noticed the number; his room or place of business must have been in the block just the other side of the used-car lot.

It was awful to know Patrick was actually lying. Neither of us had done much in that way; oh, maybe little lies to save each other when we were younger. But this was a big, serious thing. Luckily, when I got home from the tree house Patrick was coming up the driveway with Jim, so I didn't have to tell Mom he hadn't been in the tree house.

But when I showed Patrick the man's business card and handed him his arithmetic book he said angrily, "So you're still Mr. Snoopy."

"I wasn't snooping," I answered, as mad as could be. "I simply happened to find it."

"Well, keep your nose out of my business from now on!"

"I will," I said hotly. "I don't like the way it smells."

Patrick disappeared regularly with Hubert and Jim. Every day after school they went away down toward

Livernois Avenue and didn't get home till suppertime. I thought of following them with my coaster, pretending that I wanted to go to my favorite junkyard. But I didn't have the courage to try to find out what they were doing wrong.

Patrick thought up some fancy excuses to explain where he was. First it was the tree house. Then when it began to rain, and later snow, along about Thanksgiving time Mom knew they wouldn't be having any fun down there in the wet and cold. So Patrick said the three of them were doing a special Boy Scout project, and when she wanted to know what, he just said, "Christmas is coming, Mother dear. Ask me no questions, I'll tell you no lies."

My poor mother. I think by her pleased expression she must have thought Patrick was actually making her some special gift, down in the Baptist Church basement where the Scouts met. But I knew he wasn't spending his time down there either. Once I even did go past with my coaster, just to be sure I wasn't doing Patrick an injustice imagining things that were bad about him. But the church was closed up tight and the doors were all locked. So I knew he was really lying all this time.

In the meantime, I went ahead with my plans to make Christmas presents. I set up my projects at my workbench in the basement and pulled a piece of canvas over them whenever I quit for the night. I got hold of a cigar box and used my scroll saw, some varnish, and glue to make Dad a dandy pipe rack. Then I made a neat set of spice-box shelves for Mom.

Once Mom had given me a present of a wood-burning set, with an electric needle. I got a pretty piece of birch, shaped it like a shield, and made a burnt-wood plaque for Patrick. On it I did a picture of our old dog Shep, just the head. It was so good and so lifelike I almost wanted to keep it. But that's the best kind of present, one you'd like to have yourself.

Dad was making a doll house for Betsy, and he got me to wire it for electricity. We worked on it together in the evenings down in the basement. Dad was a pretty neat carpenter. He made a square four-room house on a beaverboard platform, with a red peaked roof that lifted off so Betsy and her friends could play with the dolls and furniture inside. He made an imitation chimney running up one side. It was hollow so you could hide a battery in there. A switch beside the chimney turned on the lights.

It was real good the way he had it planned.

Following the rules in my Boy Scout manual, I wired the house so that each room was lighted by a tiny dim bulb on one wall when you pressed the switch. When the lights were connected we called Mom and Patrick down to see. Mom turned on the lights so often that I grinned and said, "Careful, you'll wear out the battery."

Then Patrick wanted to help too, so Dad said, "Suppose you make the furniture."

Well, he made tiny beds, tables, and chairs just big enough for the three-inch boy and girl dolls Mom bought to live there. I had to keep hands off, though his furniture wasn't much better than just blocks of wood.

But I wasn't going to have him sore about something else, like my being handier than he was with tools.

He made a television set with a Mickey Mouse Club scene glued to the front. For the kitchen sink and stove and refrigerator he drew water taps and stove burners and switches, using waterproof ink. They weren't bad . . . for Patrick.

Charlotte made a whole set of tiny clay dishes, pots, and pans. Mom added curtains and pillows, sheets, and bedcovers. She even crocheted rag rugs and made a fringed tablecloth about the size of a postage stamp.

That was a lot of fun, all working together on Betsy's present.

During December the feeling of Christmas coming was everywhere. Along the highways trucks carried Christmas trees by the millions to markets and corner lots where they were stacked for sale. We saw them lying tied in huge clumps in the backs of trucks, their cut stumps all round and cream-colored below the dark green branches. When we went to buy our tree, the first real snow was falling, and the trees in the lot smelled so of woods with stars above that I was homesick for the cut-over country.

Mom took Betsy and me shopping for gifts downtown. She left us beside the electric trains while she went off on errands, where bright games and books, mittens and skates, were waiting to be bought. I enjoyed watching those beautiful sleek trains run through tunnels and around figure eights of track. The "reefers" had sliding doors and the gondolas had lumps of coal that could be taken out. Some of the flat cars carried

tiny car bodies, as if they were leaving Detroit factories.

Mom came back carrying odd-shaped packages, and we pushed our way through the crowds. You could smell chocolate, perfume, radiator steam, and evergreens. Enormous lighted trees with colored balls winked above our heads. Some of them turned slowly to music; some shimmered as if they were giggling. Down on the main floor near the escalator was a showcase so full of chocolates that the salesgirl could hardly get her hand in. She took some out and weighed them on white-and-gold scales.

"Gee," said Betsy, "can you imagine anything finer than waiting on candy customers?"

By Christmas Eve everything had been made, bought, wrapped, and delivered. A tree stood in a corner of our living room all lit up pretty and with plenty of packages underneath.

Mom was to sing in *The Messiah* with her church choir, and Dad took all three of us to hear it, though Patrick grumbled a good bit. When we stepped from the snow outside into the warm church, there were hundreds of lighted candles making everything glow with a halo. The walls were covered with dark green branches, and I could smell ground juniper. (I remembered how branches in woods smelled when your feet crunched on them.) Behind the candles on window sills were red berries and bows of red satin ribbon and a little bit of mistletoe.

Mom stood among the other singers in her red choir robe. I looked at the other boys and girls who had come with their parents and wondered if they liked this music. Mom had promised me that some day I probably would.

By and by the choir burst into what seemed like millions of Hallelujahs. My head jerked and I realized I had dozed. I smiled at Dad and knew that Dad's head had jerked too, as though he had waked up just in time.

Mom joined us in the church porch, and we found our way to the car. It had been raining all day, turning to snow at dusk. The sidewalks were freezing over, and there was a thin film of ice as slick as a skating rink.

"Ought to have chains tonight," said Dad.

As we drove home we could see Christmas trees in front windows all up and down the streets. Our own street was one long jagged line of steep roofs with a fringe of television aerials above. There were two Christmas trees in almost every house, one in each upstairs flat and one for the family downstairs.

Across the street before the Winslow house stood a brand-new car, wrapped completely in cellophane and tied on top with an enormous red bow. Mrs. Winslow, Larry's mother, was laughing and crying as she tried to untie the bow.

Larry's father hugged her and shouted, "Surprised, dear?"

I rushed upstairs ahead of everyone to plug in the Christmas-tree lights. When the family crossed the doorsill the little tree glowed and twinkled.

"Merry Christmas, everybody," I yelled. Then I pressed the switch beside the chimney of the doll house.

"Oh, oh, a doll house! And it lights up!" shrieked Betsy. "Oh, Dad, did you do this?" She took off the roof and with trembling hands began to touch the doll furniture.

"We all did," said Dad, "but Mike did the wiring."

Betsy was shouting. "Oh, Mike, the cunning, darling light globes, so tiny. Oh, aren't you smart!"

I wasn't listening. I was staring at a tool box all my own. The tag said, "To Mike from Dad and Patrick."

I began to lift out the tools, all things they had

picked out personally, a steel claw hammer, a hand drill, a crosscut handsaw, two screwdrivers, a block plane, a try square, a hacksaw, tin snips. If anything was lacking, I didn't know it.

I had to wipe my eyes so that the Christmas tree would stop looking double and blurry. "Golly, Dad, thanks," I said.

"And Patrick," reminded Dad.

"And me," added Patrick.

"I meant you too," I said lamely, wishing I'd given Patrick something more than the burnt-wood plaque. But he really liked it, I think.

"Old Shep!" he said, real quiet. "I'd almost forgotten him. Thanks, Mike."

Going to sleep later, I could remember Christmases when Dad had given me all kinds of things to try to get me interested in being a good sport and good at games —a volleyball, a punching bag, a trapeze to put up in the barn, even a Little Atlas Magic Muscle Builder (a pulley arrangement for lifting weights).

Now maybe he was beginning to think I could be a different kind of Mike—or even Michael. I tell you, it feels good to *know* who you are and that it's all right to be that person.

Whitey Jones, Auto Mechanic

I woke up early Christmas Day and sneaked out to the living room to look at my new tools some more.

One thing I noticed and can't help taking time to tell you, even though it hasn't anything to do with my story: That was the brightness that was all over everything that morning. I mean everything was *real bright*.

When I looked out the kitchen window as I ate some Christmas cookies with milk there were blinding diamond sparkles everywhere. Each tree and shrub was coated with ice. I don't believe in magic, so I figured it out while I ate. It had rained and then turned real cold and a layer of ice had frozen around everything.

Every twig and evergreen needle shone as if it had been painted with glass. There were fringes of icicles on the eaves of the Winslow house across the street. Blades of grass and frozen weeds in an empty lot between two houses winked as if they were made of tin.

While I was looking out the window a mail-delivery truck stopped at our curb. A man ran up the steps and rang our bell. When I got downstairs he was holding out a couple of large square envelopes addressed to Patrick and me.

"Guess that's all, son," he said, and his breath was like the steam that rises from Mom's coffeepot.

"Thanks a lot. Merry Christmas."

In our room Patrick was putting a nail in our wall to hang the plaque of Shep I'd made. We opened our envelopes together. I found a red-white-and-blue booklet entitled "Official Soap Box Derby Rule Book." A Christmas card dropped out and I picked it off the floor. On the front was a photograph of Mr. Duffy dressed as Santa Claus, with the words, "Merry Christmas to all Pontchartrain Boys from Their Truant Officer." I chuckled, knowing I was supposed to. You get used to grown-up jokes.

I turned it over and read, "Dear Michael, I found this booklet in a store and looked into it. I hope you'll enter the Derby this summer. Looks to me as if you'd have a good chance. Best regards, Andrew Duffy."

I heard a kind of snort from Patrick and saw that he had the same kind of booklet in his hands. For a second it made me sore. Didn't Mr. Duffy respect me as a special person, different from Patrick? Did he have to lump me with my twin, who could do all the many things I couldn't do—captain any kind of ball team, ride a bicycle at the park with the other guys, even ice skate and bowl? What was so good about being able to make a racer if Patrick could do it too?

Patrick didn't like being lumped with me either. "Listen to this," he said, turning over his card.

"Dear Patrick, Wouldn't it be fun if our school had two boys entered in the Soap Box Derby this summer? And twins at that! Think what fun it would be for the rest of us to watch you and Michael, each driving his own car in the race. Hope you'll think this over. Regards, Andrew Duffy."

Patrick didn't throw the booklet into our wastebasket, the way I'd half hoped he would. He laid it on the little table by his bed, and he had a thoughtful expression even while he shook his head and said, "No, it's a goofy idea."

I thought so too and was really shocked that Mr. Duffy had suggested it. Long afterwards I realized how well he understood boys. Without the feeling that I had to do better than Patrick at something, I might never have gone on and built my racer. And without that note to him from his gym teacher Patrick might never have admitted that there was a way in which I could compete with him. He was so used to being top man!

Patrick went to get his new ice skates. A near-by corner lot had been flooded, and from morning to night it was filled with skaters—just about everyone but me. Even Betsy and Charlotte went fearfully around the edge, holding crossed hands in front of them, using little chopping strokes of their feet, getting all pink around the noses while their hair flew out from under their bright wool caps. As for Dickie Fells, I'd seen him pick himself up from the ice and dust himself off so many times I would have thought he'd quit; but he can be stubborn.

Well, I curled up on the living-room couch, where I could look at the Christmas tree, and read the booklet while my teeth crunched into one of the pink-fleshed snow apples Grandma had sent.

"Since 1933," I read, "the Derby has been a national event for boys. The final race takes place in Akron, Ohio. Last year about a hundred and fifty boys from all over the country, even from Alaska and Ireland, competed in the finals. But before the race in Akron there were races in all important cities to pick the finalists."

I began to get excited as I turned the pages full of pictures and printed directions. In the middle of the book was a double-page, colored, lettered diagram showing the detail of steering and brake assemblies.

I got an old school notebook I'd once kept for making notes on butterflies around Manton. I left the butterfly notes in, but turned the notebook around backward and wrote at the top of the first page, "Rules for making a Soap Box Derby racer." All the time I was reading and writing down the rules for myself I could smell the turkey cooking and hear, like background music, Mom and Dad making a long-distance call to Grandma and Uncle Horace and Aunt Suzy to say Merry Christmas.

Here's my list:

1. Do all work myself (but okay to have a machine-shop drill steering shaft where bolts will go to lock it in place).

2. Keep record of all expenses; buy official wheels and axles.

3. No loose material.

4. No welding, brazing, or soldering.

5. Attach steering shaft to top of racer, no upright support from floor board.

6. Only brake allowed is single drag brake in center, worked by foot pedal.

I studied the diagram carefully. First I must work out my steering assembly, then the brake assembly, and finally the upholstering and body covering. I decided to put in a seat with a hinged back that could be tilted forward so the inside might be inspected. I would have to upholster the cockpit. Maybe Jim Hoyt would get me some of his father's old sample materials cheap.

The combined weight of car and driver must not be over 250 pounds. I weigh light myself, barely a hundred when I jump up and down on the scales to drive the pointer up a bit. I knew that if I added to the weight of my racer, it would hold the road better. So I decided I would make hardwood axletrees, two leaves to each with the axle fitted between.

I made a careful list of the amount of oak lumber I would need for axletrees, brake pedal and brake shoe, and bulkheads. (I included, too, enough wood for the floor board, but that was before Mrs. Hoyt gave me her old ironing board. I'll tell about that later.) I even listed finally the number of hinges, turnbuckles, pulleys, and bolts I had to buy.

Well, you can see that getting that rule book was mighty important to me. The other important thing

that happened on Christmas Day was that I met
Whitey Jones.

After a great big Christmas dinner Patrick went ice
skating again.

Me? I took my old coaster and went for a long
walk. And so I met Whitey Jones, an auto mechanic
with a shop so much like Smitty's Garage in Manton
that at last, at last, I felt at home in Detroit.

The snow had melted off the streets, but it was
still packed hard in banks along the curbs. It was good
pulling that old coaster and going for a long walk
by myself. I went farther than usual. Maybe you feel
sorry for me, wandering all alone on Christmas Day
when the other kids were skating. Well, you needn't.
I was perfectly happy. I had always liked walking
alone in the cut-over country around home; and now
I'd made up my mind that this great big city was home
too.

I especially liked filling stations. Every few blocks
in any direction I had discovered I would find a corner
area of concrete hosed clean, with three or four gasoline pumps and a little business house all shiny with
glass and fresh paint. There were always two or three
young men in uniforms, filling gas tanks and cleaning
windshields. Sometimes I'd talk to the guys, but they
didn't seem to know too much. I mean, all they did
was clean and service the cars. They couldn't have
straightened out troubles the way Smitty did.

Well, the day I met Whitey Jones I kept walking
and walking. I thought, I'll turn back when I get to
the next filling station. I was at least a mile from home

and the sun was setting when I saw a big sign painted black and white: "Whitey Jones, Auto Mechanic."

This was different from the other filling stations I'd seen. It was at the edge of a trailer village. Three red gasoline pumps and a little glass-and-metal office stood on a square of concrete. Around it the rest of the lot was hard-packed dirt, and under a willow tree in one corner was an old shed with its door sagging open, almost like our tool shed on the farm.

That shed took my eye, so I went over and peeked in. It was full of tools lying around as if someone used them all the time, not too clean, not very orderly. A man in dirty overalls was sharpening a tool on a grinder. He was so busy he didn't seem to notice the shriek of metal on stone nor the shower of sparks around him in the dark shed.

I stood there holding the rope of my coaster, staring at him. It was like having found Smitty's Garage for the first time. Behind the shed I could see lights coming on in all the trailers. There must have been a hundred of them, each one a home smaller than the place we lived in.

I could hear children's noises and mothers calling. A baby cried somewhere near-by, and the man looked up from his work. He saw me. "Well, hello," said Whitey Jones.

Seeing as how he was friendly, I moved in and walked around not touching things, just looking, like you do in a museum.

"Hi," I said finally. "This is a keen place."

"Thanks. I'd show you around, but it's pretty late and I suppose your mother is worrying about you."

"She doesn't worry much," I said. I guess he was sort of scolding me, but I was too interested in all his tools to notice.

The man turned off the grinder and laid down the tool. "Say, I need a boy around here sometimes. Ever wash your dad's car?"

"Not alone, but I've helped."

"Well, maybe you could help me." He laughed, and I think this must have been because I looked so tickled. I began to tell him about my dad's work in an auto factory and about the new tool box I'd got for Christmas. In two minutes I felt as if I'd known him forever. So I wasn't surprised that he felt the same way. At least he must have, or he wouldn't have asked me to supper the way he did.

"Long as you're here," he said, "we've got a steak big enough for four. Reckon you could phone your mother and stay? It's suppertime and I'm hungry."

"Steak on Christmas?" This was strange.

In the fast-going light I could see that, while most of the trailers were white or yellow or silvery, the one behind this man's shop was sky-blue, with red-striped awnings and geraniums at the windows. When we got inside, there was a young woman pushing spoonfuls of food into a baby. Now I could see the man real well in the bright light.

He was long and thin, with long clever-looking hands. His face was long and thin too, what Dad would call a horsy face, and a lock of white hair fell across his forehead. His cheeks were leathery, brown as if from years of sun and creased with deep smiles.

"I don't know your name," said Whitey.

"I'm Mike. Michael Williams."

"Okay, Mike, first phone your Mom."

Well, what do you know, Mom was worried, after all! She was so mad I was embarrassed for fear Whitey could hear her sputtering. By and by I managed to interrupt her. "I'm sorry, Mom, honest; but I met this new friend and he wants me to stay to supper."

More sputtering! "How do you know he isn't a . . . a city slicker?" That made me mad; she'd never suspected Patrick of getting into trouble. But just let me do one thing out of line!

Whitey took the phone and said very seriously, "Look, Mrs. Williams, I know how you feel, believe me. He was my kid, I'd lam him clear from here to China for running off. But long as he's here, we'd like him to share a steak with us. I'll bring him home right after, in my pickup. Yes, ma'am."

So I got my way, but felt rather funny for a while.

I had never been inside a trailer before, so he showed me around while his wife started fixing dinner.

I was surprised to see how much you could get into such a little space. At one end were a stove and sink and a table hardly bigger than my coaster. The table had a red-checked cover and there were red-and-white curtains at the windows.

At the other end was a gray couch and a television set. All around the walls were shelves of books and dishes. Lying on a gun rack above the door was a deer rifle. Whitey kept opening little doors here and there to show me drawers and closets full of fishing and camping equipment.

"We like to travel light," he said. "Go up to the Upper Peninsula in summer, sometimes join the berry pickers."

"Where do you sleep?" I asked.

Whitey did something to the couch so quickly I couldn't see it, and now it was a full-sized bed. He turned it back into a couch again just by touching a button.

I had never had more pure fun than I did talking

to Whitey over the steak and potatoes. I told him first about what it was like on our farm, and before I knew it I even told him I'd played hookey a whole week and was on a year's probation with the school truant officer. He didn't seem as shocked as his wife did. She got up and cleared the table and gave us some apple pie and went to put their baby to bed.

Whitey told me how he and his brother had once made a sidewalk car driven by a real gas engine. "My dad gave us an old washing-machine motor no one could make run any more. That was all we needed to get us going." I don't remember all about it, but I could tell that he was a genius when it came to making things go.

And suddenly I knew here was a man who could help me if I got stuck building a racer.

"I want to build a coaster to enter in the Soap Box Derby next summer," I told him after a while.

"Nothing to it," he assured me.

"Well, I wouldn't say that. I've been reading the rule book and I put down a lot of directions to myself. But I have to work out a steering assembly and a brake assembly like in the diagram. And I'm not always so good at following rules."

"Then high time you learned," said Whitey, standing up. "And the rule you've got to learn before you're any older is, 'Always be home before dark.' Come on now!"

I Build My Racer

Guess who was in the basement the day after Christmas when I got down to my workbench? Mrs. Hoyt.

She was peeling layers of padding off an old ironing board and stuffing them into the furnace.

"Well, hello, Mike," she greeted me. "Did you have a good Christmas?"

Like most grown-ups she didn't really listen for an answer, but went on jabbering about her own affairs: "I got a brand new ironer from my husband. What do you think of that?"

"Gee," I said in some embarrassment, "is that what you wanted?" (It seemed a dull enough present, to me.)

She laughed, shaking all over a little. All the Hoyts are fat. "Sure it is. What did you get?"

"Oh, I got this keen tool set." I began to show her, but I could see that she didn't care any more about my tool box than I did about her ironer. Good night!

"Say," she said, running her hand down over the smooth wood of the old ironing board, "I wonder if

129

you could use this, Mike. It's no use to me any more."

Could I? I remembered the directions in the Derby Rule Book, something like this—"Floorboard of wood only, about ¾ of an inch thick." This would be exactly right. I could see myself cutting it down, making a teardrop-shaped floor for a racing car—square across the rear and tapered to a rounded point in front.

"Can I really have it, Mrs. Hoyt?" It was pretty wood, the color and smoothness of beeswax.

"Sure. I'm glad to get rid of it."

"Maybe I should pay you something for it." I remembered reading in the rules about keeping track of costs of materials.

"Are you crazy, boy? Take it and welcome."

Well, that was the beginning of my racer.

I'll tell you right now the hardest thing I had to learn was to be accurate, mathematically accurate. You look at a bunch of racers and they all look almost alike. But there's a world of difference in the way they run; and the best-built car has a lot better chance of winning the race, even if you're lopsided personally—like me. I knew I wouldn't be able to drive my racer as easily as a lot of other guys on account of my right side not being so good.

So I worked more carefully than I'd ever done on anything in my life. I remembered Dad had had to show me how a kingpin helped to give my old coaster steerability (he had called it a carriage bolt, but it was the same thing). This time I was determined not to ask Dad anything. I'd surprise him and Mr. Duffy and everybody by doing the thing right.

Meantime I had my new friend, Whitey Jones. I can't tell you how good it made me feel to know he was out there in his shop at the edge of the trailer village. I knew he'd help me figure out anything I needed advice on, but he'd see to it that I did it alone as I was supposed to do. I knew from the way he'd scolded me for staying out after dark that he wouldn't let me skimp on any rules.

First I had to buy my wheels and axles, an "official" set. I shook all the money from my Mexican pig bank, and taking my old coaster, went over to Livernois Avenue.

Here in the store where I had seen last year's Derby winner I bought a set of official wheels and axles. I really believed in myself by that time, and my heart was light. It was as if I was running on a track I had made for myself.

I went on down the street to my favorite junkyard. There I found a steering wheel and shaft. It was lying almost hidden by a tall mullein plant—a shiny black plastic wheel with three spokes. About ten inches in diameter, it was firmly attached to a shaft a little over fifteen inches long. It had probably been used in some wartime radar equipment.

I took it to the man in the warehouse next door. "How much for this old thing?" I asked.

"Well-ll, let's say a dollar, kid."

"I'll take it."

Back in the basement I sawed out the top third of the rim. (When I crouched over the wheel to drive the racer my chin would just fit the V-shaped space between the spokes.) I filed the sawed edges smooth and wrapped them with black masking tape. Then I washed the wheel and worked over it with polishing wax until it looked good as new.

That took pretty nearly all day while the other kids were skating and having a taffy-pull at Emmy Jo's. I'd like to have gone to that, but no one had asked me.

It still bothered me that Patrick and Jim and Hubert went off together a lot toward Livernois. I hadn't seen them over there the day I bought my wheels, because that was the day of Emmy Jo's taffy-pull. But just about every day it seemed to me they were either going off, all three, on some mysterious errand, or coming back looking sort of tired and secretive.

But I couldn't do anything about that; at least I told myself I couldn't. And I'll bet most anyone would have decided the same thing. You just can't approach a brother (a twin, even) and say, "Look here, come clean. What's up?"

So I worked hard and tried not to wonder what was going on.

I made a lot of extra trips out to Whitey's place during those two weeks of holiday, partly to consult him, partly just to see him and smell the good shop where he worked. He lent me his jack plane to shape the body and axletrees of my racer.

I spent a whole afternoon shaping the ironing board into a beautiful tear-drop pattern, with pointed nose and blunt rear. Then I spent all evening shaping the leaves of the axletrees. I loved the feel of the satiny wood I had bought at the nearest lumber yard. Then I bolted each axle between its two leaves.

Next I measured the floor board and located the right spot for the drag brake. With my keyhole saw I cut out a block that left just the right-sized hole for the brake.

Now I made my bulkheads and hinged them, front and back, to the floor board. In the middle of the two front bulkheads I drilled holes for the steering shaft. I marked the shaft where the locking bolts would go.

The rule book said I could have help getting the shaft drilled for the locking bolts; and I could have the axles machined too, the front axle for the kingpin and the back axle for bolts to fasten it to the chassis. So I loaded them onto my coaster and away I went to

Whitey's shop. (I should have told you long ago that I had put sides around my coaster so it would haul more junk.)

I went to the trailer village by way of alleys trimmed with fascinating discarded junk for the city to cart away. Every time I came to someone's ash can or incinerator I'd look over what hadn't been burned to see if there was anything I could use.

As I walked along, pulling my coaster, the houses came to life. Back doors slammed, voices called from doorways, washing machines in basements made noises of splash and whirl, and somewhere a dog barked.

I found Whitey in front of his shop, stretching his arms in the morning sunshine. He grinned at me and was tickled to death to drill the holes in the steering shaft and axles.

His smile creases were deep, and his eyes twinkled when he asked, "What else can I do you for?" I think by now he'd begun to think helping me was almost as good as building a racer himself. But we were terribly careful, right through, that I got only the "legal," allowable help.

"I noticed you've got a great big roll of airplane cable, Whitey—looks like about a sixteenth inch. Could I buy some for my steering cable?"

"Sure thing. Why not take the whole roll? Measure off what you need when you get to it and bring the rest back. We'll figure out the price on the basis of footage. Okay?"

"Fine."

"Sounds like you've got things under control."

"Well, so far, at least."

Now every day saw a little bit more work done. I bolted my rear axle to the car floor and put on the front axle. When I put the kingpin down through the floor board and the front axle, I had to smile, remembering when Dad had "treated" me to a carriage bolt for my first coaster in Manton.

I rolled the little racer back and forth on its beautiful wheels. It was really taking shape. It "went" now. Wheels are a wonderful invention! What did people do without them?

I kept my instruction sheet right in front of me. I threaded the steering shaft through the bulkheads and locked it into position with bolts where Whitey had drilled the holes.

Now I bolted one end of the airplane cable to the front axle. Then I fastened a pulley to the car floor and used it to guide the cable onto the steering shaft. I put another pulley opposite, to guide the other end of the cable to the other end of the axle.

But I had gone too fast and had wrapped the steering cable around the shaft in the wrong direction. When I turned the steering wheel it steered backwards!

Well, no time to get disgusted with myself. I had to learn patience, like that spider I'd watched in the fall reweaving his web. I unthreaded the cable back to the steering column and rolled it in the opposite direction.

When I had done that, I turned the steering wheel from side to side. It obeyed me by turning the front wheels the way I wanted them to go. But there was too much play in the wheel. I cut the cable and put in a turnbuckle at either end, just above where it was fastened to the axle. I wired each turnbuckle to prevent its ever unwinding.

"Now for the brake assembly," I said. I'd begun talking to myself sometimes while I worked, but no one heard me. And if they had, I wouldn't have cared. I knew I not only wasn't crazy, but I was also doing something none of those other guys had bothered to figure out for himself! I felt good.

I made another trip out to Whitey's to get a slice of truck-tire tread. I figured it would be the perfect facing for my drag brake. I went over the diagram carefully, then went to work with the happy feeling that I knew what I was about.

First I faced the brake shoe with the piece of tire tread. Then I hinged the foot pedal at the front of the chassis, just where my foot could push it to the floor when I wanted to stop the car or slow it down.

Now I fastened eyebolts to the floor. Through them I guided the brake cable to the rear. Here at the square hole I'd sawed in the floor I hinged three blocks of wood in such a way that when I pushed the brake pedal in front, the cable opened up the two top blocks like a book. This action pushed down the third block (hinged in the opposite direction) so that the rubber brake facing would grip the road. This third block bobbed from the rear bulkhead on a looped screen-door spring, clear of the road unless I used the front pedal. When my foot floored this brake pedal it would push the brake hard down against the road to slow the car.

Finally I had the whole assembly completed. It was

by now the last day of our Christmas vacation, about four in the afternoon. I sat down on the car floor (where I would build and upholster a seat later). I turned the front wheels this way and that, putting my face close to the steering wheel where the top V had been cut out and making soft *bzz-zzumm* noises. Then I pushed the brake pedal and down went the brake, gripping the floor.

"It works," I said to myself with deep satisfaction.

For once not shy, I ran out and down to the skating rink.

"Come see my racer," I yelled.

Everyone stopped and looked at me. "Come on," said Jimmie Hoyt, grinning. "Must be something wonderful." He began to take off his skates.

When Jimmie saw the racer his eyes opened wide and wider. I let him sit in it and turn the steering wheel and push the brake. Patrick and the others stood around, looking kind of amazed.

Jim whistled. "Gee, it works good, Mike. Show me how to make one, will ya, huh?"

"That's real neat," said Richard Depew.

Patrick said not a word, even when I said, "Wanta look her over, Pat?"

All the girls murmured, "It's not very pretty."

"Oh, for goodness' sake," said Hubert, "all you girls think about is how things look."

"It works, that's the thing," pointed out Larry Winslow. "Wish we had a hill to try it on."

"We could take it out to Middle Rouge Park some day and try it," suggested Jim. "There's a hill there."

"I'm going to," I said. "Whitey—my friend Whitey Jones—promised to take it out on his truck some Sunday so I can practice driving it. I'm going to drive it in the Soap Box Derby."

"Are you, honest?"

"But this doesn't look—"

"It isn't finished yet. I'm going to make the prettiest body cover I can think of and upholster it inside. Then I have to true up the steering and check all the rules again for size and weight."

"I always wanted to be in the Derby when I got old enough," said Jimmie.

Still not a sound out of Patrick! For once I'd got the drop on him, and again I had a feeling he almost hated me. But I couldn't have cared less right then.

I glanced down at my little car. Lovingly I patted one of the wheels and ran my hand around the tire. "No reason you shouldn't be in the race," I said to Jim, "except one. You weigh too much. Rule says car and driver can't total over 250 pounds."

The other guys gave him a horse laugh. Jim muttered, "I'll reduce." (I guess he knew he never could give up anything good to eat, and his mother is a very good cook who throws butter into everything.)

"You're allowed by the rules to team up to build a racer," I suggested, because I began to feel sorry for Pat. "Pat and Jim could build one together, and Pat could race it."

At last Patrick spoke. "Mr. Duffy suggested Mike and I might both build racers and be in the Derby together."

Jim looked down his nose. "You'd need my help, Patrick," he said. "You couldn't do this good a job."

"Huh." Patrick said no more. He knew Jim was right.

"Come on," said Charlotte impatiently. "Let's have a game of kick-the-can before supper." But when the others ran out she touched the wheels all around and said quietly, "It's real nice, Mike. Makes you feel good, huh?"

The City Slicker Vanishes

February is probably the worst school month anywhere, but it was especially bad in Detroit that year. Everything was frozen solid, and the world was so cold that even our basement close to the furnace was never really warm.

I tried to believe in the reality of summer and the plans I had, but I was tired of working so hard. So I pulled a canvas over my racer and let it rest for a while.

It was so cold that the wind whistled at the storm windows as though it would tear them off. Snow whirled down day after day and buried our street under sparkling white.

Then the cold spell broke, and there were days of slush underfoot, with rain washing away the dirty snow banks along the sidewalks. Instead of skating on the corner rink, the guys began a mud fight that lasted one whole weekend. I got in on that too and threw as much mud as anyone else. Boy, were our folks all mad. It was fun for me, being scolded along with the others.

In classrooms there were sneezy new colds, snuffly old ones, colds that threatened to become pneumonia, others that were just bad enough to make excuses to stay home.

But Pat got really sick. I still don't believe he would ever have entered the Soap Box Derby with me if he hadn't been so sick that winter.

He must have been coming down with this "strep throat" on a Saturday, because he not only turned down an invitation to go to a double-feature movie with Hubert and Mildred Lucile, but that night he said No when Dad asked him to go bowling! And the next morning he said he didn't believe he could go to Sunday school. I might have thought this was just an excuse, but since Emmy Jo was going to give a report I didn't think he'd want to miss unless he really felt bad.

"My throat hurts awful, Mom," he complained, and Mom put her hand to his forehead just like she would have put out a hand to stop her alarm clock from ringing. But the alarm started after she felt his forehead. She jerked her hand away and jumped up saying, "Frank, he's got a high fever. Call the doctor!"

Betsy and I went off mighty solemn with Emmy Jo when she came by, and I could see she was disappointed that Patrick wasn't going. When we came home the doctor was leaving, and I heard him say, "Better get the other boy out of there. Can you make a bed in the living room?"

"Is it that bad?" The weight of fear in Mom's voice scared me more than anything had up to then.

"It's very contagious, that's all. If the boy's in good physical condition otherwise, I think drugs will bring him out of this in a few days. But he may need to take it easy for a while afterwards."

I stopped worrying at once. Boys my age like to have things laid on the line, and the doctor had done that. So I helped Dad open out the couch into a bed and then carried my clothes and books out of the bedroom, and thought it rather a lark, even though Mom looked so worried. It seemed funny putting my clothes into the desk drawers, but I got used to being out there that first day.

Later, Mom sent me to the drugstore to pick up a prescription, and there was the city slicker, Harry Bonham, sitting in his car at the curb.

He looked hard at me and, I guess, realized that I was Patrick's twin. "Hey, kid," he called, "C'mere."

I didn't like going over to talk to him. But I knew Pat was somehow mixed up with him so I went.

"You Pat Williams's brudda?" he asked, and I nodded.

"Well, I expected to see him here at t'ree o'clock. Where'n Sam Hill is he, I wanta know?"

"My brother is sick," I said, anxious to get away.

"No kiddin'. Well, that's a fine pickle he leaves me in. D'you know if he's got a little book wit' a lot o' loose papers stuck in it, a little red book that says 'Accounts' on front?"

"No, I don't. He told me to keep my nose out of his

business. I gotta go now, gotta get a prescription filled."

I moved away, trying not to seem in a hurry. But he called after me, "Tell Hoyt when you get back home I wanta see him here pronto, you hear?"

"Okay, I will." It was a relief to get into the drugstore that smelled so good and so innocent of trouble. It smelled like Charlotte's mother when she goes for a violin lesson. I read some comic books till the prescription was ready. That guy was still at the curb when I got out. I was afraid he'd offer to drive me home in the rain, but I guess he didn't want to be seen on our street. It was just around the corner and up two blocks anyway, and I much preferred to walk.

Mom wouldn't let me in Patrick's room so I couldn't have looked for that red account book if I'd wanted to.

But I knew I had to get that message to Jim. Otherwise the man might get in touch with my folks, and I didn't want Pat in more trouble than the strep throat was causing him. So I phoned Jim, since I knew he wouldn't want his folks to know about this man either. Over the phone I said, "Hey, Jim, how's about meeting me down at my workbench in the basement? I wanta show you something."

It worked, and we both got down there at the same time. I told him, "Some character is waiting over by the drugstore to see you, Jim. He wanted me to get hold of an account book Pat's supposed to have, but I can't lay my hands on it. Mom won't let me in the bedroom because the doctor said Pat's contagious."

Jim kept looking down at his foot, which was pushing circles around on the concrete floor as if trying to write an answer to a bad puzzle. "Gosh, Mike, you oughta find that book if you possibly can. I don't trust that guy if we can't show him our figures in black and white."

Then I came out with all the worry I'd been feeling for the last few months. The next day (March 1) I was to report to the truant officer for the sixth time, and I'd made a perfect record so far. But I didn't think I could keep from telling Mr. Duffy about Pat if he was really in serious trouble; I knew by now that Mr. Duffy was there to help us, even if it meant we had to take some punishment.

"Jim, what's that guy into you fellows for?" I demanded.

He looked up at me then, and I could see he was

surprised. "You mean to say Patrick never told you?" he said.

"Pat never tells me anything any more," I said bitterly. When I stopped to think about it I very much minded his having secrets with other guys and not me. I went on, quite angry, "I know I wouldn't trust that fellow any farther than I could throw him with my right hand, and my right hand ain't so good."

"Well, maybe you're right, but we all wanted to earn some money, and our folks wouldn't let us have paper routes. I think they should've."

"Yeah, so do I." I couldn't help siding with him on that. But I was scared to death of what he was going to tell me.

"Anyway, this guy persuaded us to get magazine subscriptions for him every day after school for a couple of hours."

I felt so dizzy with relief I grabbed at the edge of the workbench. "Magazine subscriptions?"

Jim leaned back against the bench and folded his arms. "Well, yes," he said, glancing at me in a funny way. "What did you think we were doing, stealing hub caps and peddling cigarettes?"

All I could do was nod. And when he didn't hear any answer he looked at me and saw me nodding like a fool, like one of those silly birds you can get in a Trick-and-Stunt store that balances back and forth and dips its beak into a glass of water. I just kept nodding and couldn't say a word.

Jim was pretty mad. He hit his flat hand down hard on the bench beside him. "Well, I like that!" he scolded.

"You honestly think us guys would go for some crooked racket?"

"Jim, I didn't know what to think. I found this man's card in Pat's arithmetic book one time and when I asked him about it Pat got mad and told me to mind my own business. The truant officer had shown me all these files of fellows from our school who got into trouble, either in gangs or all alone, and that man sure looked like trouble to me, if I ever met it. And remember the time I came to the tree house and you guys hid your smokes? How'd I know they weren't doped?"

"Oh, for gosh sakes, Mike, seems like you could've trusted us."

"I don't know about that. I bet you wouldn't have trusted me."

He didn't answer and I knew he was feeling bad about the way things had gone among us that winter. "Why did you tell Mr. Duffy on us for smoking, Mike?"

I blew up then. "I never did tell him. You just thought I did."

"Well . . . who did tell him?"

"Some girl, he said—maybe Hubert's sister found some cigarettes in his bedroom. Gosh, do you guys just have to think I'm a stinker?"

He looked pretty guilty, so I got over being mad right quick. "What kind of magazines did you get subscriptions for?" I wanted to know.

"Oh, all of 'em. Gee whiz, Mike, there was nothing phoney about that! We didn't take money for subscriptions; people sent their checks and money orders directly to Mr. Bonham. Only there's an ordinance against house-to-house selling so we couldn't solicit in this neighborhood. He took us over in his car to Hamtramck——"

"Where?"

"Hamtramck, where lots of Polish people live."

"Oh, yeah, I know."

"Then we'd go up and down the streets, get subscriptions to all the popular magazines. We did real well, but Patrick kept all the records because he's the best of the three of us at figures."

"Mean to say that Mr. Bonham didn't keep records too?"

"Yeah, that's what worries me for fear his don't agree with ours. If I can't take him Patrick's book, he can tell me anything about how much he owes us, whether it's true or not."

"Hasn't he paid you anything yet?"

"Oh, yeah, he paid us up to Christmas. But he's been puttin' us off ever since. We were gettin' tired of the deal."

"Well, Jim, won't you have to tell all the folks by and by? They'll wonder where you guys get your extra money, especially if Pat cuts loose and buys a bicycle this spring."

"Oh, I don't know. It seemed like a lark when we started. But once we were into it we got a little scared. My folks won't like it a bit that I've been deceiving them about all those hours I was supposed to be doing Boy Scout projects. They might even cut off my privileges, and that would mean no Little League for me this summer."

I thought it would serve Jim right if his folks got mad, even if the fellows hadn't been doing anything illegal. It seemed to me it was wrong to lie about where you'd been spending your time. When I'd played hookey I came clean after a week of it and told—but, to be honest, I might not have told if I hadn't been seen by Mrs. Hoyt.

Well, Jim dashed out to see that Harry Bonham— only Mr. Bonham wasn't by the drugstore when he got there. Jim was on his bicycle, with his white Deputy Boy slicker and sou'wester on, so he rode on down to this man's address on Livernois.

And you know what he found? The guy had cleared out that very day. He'd been waiting to get the final report from Pat when he just decided he'd better move on to some other address.

Jim came back and I saw him ride up the street to Hubert's house. Then the two of them came down to our basement, and I went down to represent Patrick. They didn't question my being there. They just looked up when I came in and said, "Hi, Mike. That devil, looks like he flew the coop."

"How much did he owe you?" I wanted to be able to tell Patrick as soon as he was well enough.

"Well, Patrick's got the book, but it must have been about eleven dollars apiece."

"Good night."

"Yeah, that's what I say."

Pat's fever didn't go down very fast, maybe because he'd been going it too hard and he wasn't actually in

very good condition. Anyway, one night he was deliri-
ous and began calling for Dad. When Dad went to him
Pat said, "It wasn't anything, Dad, nothing at all. Just
that we had to say, 'Good day, ma'am,'" and then he
got all mixed up and began to cry hard. Poor Dad came
out of the bedroom wringing wet with sweat and looking scared.

I had to tell him what I knew, and then he went back
and kept stroking Patrick's forehead saying, "It's all
right, son, it's all right." I could hear him and it made
me feel bad clear down in, but good too. You know
what I mean? As if things might have been a lot worse
if they hadn't stopped right when they did.

Another thing that happened that night was that
Pat wanted me. Mom stayed in with him during the
worst times; and she came out to say, "Mike, your
brother wants to talk to you."

I went into the dark room and stood just inside the
door—Mom said I'd better not go too near, but he was
so sick she couldn't deny him a chance to talk to his
own twin.

"Mike," he said in a voice sort of small and way down
inside him, "you never tattled on us."

"I never did, Patrick," I answered strong and quiet.

"I didn't think so. Hubert thought you did, but I
said No."

I could feel tears running down inside my throat.
"You were right," I told him. "You just get well, Patrick.
Don't worry about anything. Everything's okay."

"Yeah." The same faraway voice. It scared me.

"Yeah," he repeated, a little stronger. "You're a good guy." It was not much more than a whisper, but I know that's what he said. "So long, Mike."

When Patrick began to get better the thing he talked most about was being cheated out of twelve dollars. He found the account book and showed me he had earned that much on commissions, while Jim and Hubert had only totted up nine or ten.

"It would have been enough, with what I already have, to get a secondhand bicycle anyway," he wept. "I was ready to quit the job. That guy used to make me feel uncomfortable, like we weren't doing an honest thing."

"Well, Pat—you gotta admit it isn't honest lying to the folks."

"Where do you get off calling me Pat all the time?"

"I don't know," I answered quietly. "I just feel like it."

The doctor had been right about Pat's needing a while to recover from the sickness, and he repeated this the last time he came. "Let him stay around the house to rest for a week before he goes back to school," he suggested.

The lucky stiff, I thought.

So that's how it happened Patrick began going down into the basement to look over my racer and to think about maybe being in the Derby. Besides the sickness, the fact he'd been in the doghouse with my folks over lying to them about that job made him act very subdued these days.

One afternoon he said to Jim, "How's about it, Jim, would it be so hard to make a racer like Mike's?"

"You mean you or me?" asked Jim suspiciously.

"Well, I mean . . . together. We'd be a team, but I'd drive it in the race. Heck, Jim, you know I'd be most likely to win. Mike says you're too fat to qualify."

"Yeah, I know. No, it wouldn't be hard if we followed the rules—and maybe Mike would help." Jim looked at me.

What could I do but agree? "Okay," I said. "I'll help if you really want me to."

Jim and Pat Team Up Against Me

Patrick and Jim started their racer the very next week. At first Pat wanted to do everything exactly the way I'd done mine. He had no confidence at all in his ability to make things. He even wanted to find someone's old ironing board to shape into a chassis floor board! But pretty soon Jim had figured out how they could buy enough lumber for the whole job, and Pat went along with him to get it.

"You want your car a little lighter than Mike's," Jim explained, as they started out. "He weighs less than you so he needs the heavy floor and bulkheads and double axle leaves. But you want to streamline yours wherever you can."

When we told Mr. Duffy about it at the Scout meeting, on Tuesday night, I thought he looked a little worried. (And this made me mad; I was afraid he was protecting me again!) "Well, of course it's all right for you to team up," he agreed. "I had thought maybe Patrick would race you, Mike. I never thought he'd want help on making his racer, though."

"We think it'll be fun this way," said Patrick, sticking out his lower lip a bit. He wasn't going to admit in front of all the other scouts that he wasn't as good as I was at making things.

It was soon clear that Patrick didn't understand the principles of the racer's design at all. I would have been glad to explain them, but he was too proud to ask me. So I just listened to him and Jim talking it all over. I was finishing my racer while they worked on theirs. I was surprised how quick Jim picked up the main idea from the diagrams; and it was a pleasure to hear him going over it patiently with Pat. It struck me that Jim was a very patient boy and good-tempered, like so many fat kids seem to be.

It was pretty confusing working down in the basement now. Kids had left me alone while I was doing the hard part of figuring out the steering and brake assemblies. But now they were down there all the time. Jim and Patrick were too popular for their own good. Sometimes roughhousing interrupted their work for hours. Larry and Richard brought their Monopoly and Parcheesi games down, and even Emmy Jo and Mildred Lucile began to hang around watching.

I got sore . . . I could see they weren't taking it seriously enough. "Why don't you tell the other kids to stay out till you get it farther along?" I asked Jim one afternoon when we were knocking off to go up to supper.

Patrick heard me. "Matter, you jealous?" he asked.

"No, I don't think so." But I wondered. "Well—" I shrugged, "it's your racer."

"How we make the car isn't as important as how we race it," he said, grinning. "They don't have race-car drivers make their own cars in the big races. It's the driver that's the important one."

"Says you," said Jim. I wouldn't have blamed him if he'd quit on Patrick. But he was having too much fun. It did me good to see that there was another boy around there who liked to make things too.

While Jim worked out their problems and Patrick bent over and peered and got in the way and said, "Oh, yes, *now* I see," I spent careful hours finishing my car body. I hinged a seat-back to the floor board and tacked padding all around inside the cockpit.

I shaped a streamlined body out of wrapping paper. Then I laid this pattern on the chicken wire I had found in the empty lot across from school. I cut the wire mesh to fit the pattern and fastened it down smoothly over the bulkheads, tacking it firmly to my floor board. Now I smeared flour paste on spread-out newspapers and laid them over the wire frame until, with a final coating of paste, the whole thing looked like a hornet's nest.

I was ready at this point to upholster the seat and back.

"Your dad got any upholstery samples I might buy?" I asked Jim. And that evening he came down to the workbench with the prettiest dark red leather, a big piece of it. "This do?" he said.

"Say, that's beautiful. Sure you don't want it?"

"Naw, I've got an idea I want ours all green and white. Dad's got some green leather for me. He wants you to have this, though, for free; says that's his part of the fun, to supply the inside trim."

So I smoothed out that pretty red stuff and fitted it to the seat and seat-back and trimmed it as carefully as I could and tacked it on. Now came the final trick of my body construction. I stretched canvas snugly over the whole and tacked it neatly underneath so that it fit the tear-drop shape as smartly as a kid glove fits a hand. I slit a section of old garden hose and used this to edge the cockpit, wiring it down carefully. Then I gave the complete job a coat of paint as orange as a pumpkin.

"Looks like Cinderella's coach before her fairy god-mother came along," laughed Betsy.

"Everything reminds you of fairies," said Patrick.

"Not bad, Mike," said Jim thoughtfully, looking it over.

After that I could see that Patrick was going too fast, trying to catch up with me. He couldn't stand being behind me on anything. One evening he and Jim were working on their brake assembly, and I was showing them how mine went.

I showed them how the front brake pedal went down to the floor when I stepped on it so that the brake cable opened up the two blocks of wood like a book. This pushed the third block lined with tire tread against the floor and made it grip firmly.

"See how that third block bobs from the back bulkhead on a loop of screen-door spring," I said, showing them. "That spring keeps the brake block clear of the road unless I use the brake pedal at the front." I showed them several times how the spring stretched when I floored the brake pedal with my foot.

"Oh, yes, I see now," said Patrick impatiently. "Come on, Hoyt, let's get this finished up tonight. Got a screen-door spring?"

Jim laughed sarcastically. "Now, I just don't happen to have a screen-door spring on me," he said.

But Pat would not be put off. "How about the one on the door to the driveway?"

"But, Pat—" I was really horrified. "You can't use an *old* screen-door spring. It wouldn't have the right stiffness. It might give just when it shouldn't. Wait and buy one at the hardware store like I did."

"Oh, come off it, Mike. What's the difference?"

Jim was looking at the spring on the screen door that opened onto the driveway. "This is okay, I guess," he said worriedly. "Dad put this on last summer when the old one lost its zing and the door wouldn't close right."

"Well, I'd get a brand-new one," I said righteously.

"Why?" snapped Pat. "Just because it's shiny black? Who'll ever know the difference? Come on, Hoyt, unscrew it. We'll get a new one for the door when summer comes."

Patrick just didn't have the right attitude.

"And the way you've wound your steering cable," I said a day or so later. "Why, it's sloppy. Whitey says you must make everything 'eye sweet.'"

"Oh, Whitey, Whitey. You're sore because I'm going to race you, and you're afraid I'll win."

Well, that was true enough. So I didn't say any more. The next time I tried to point out they were being careless about something Pat shouted, "Oh, go fly a kite," so I did.

It was kite-flying weather by then, being almost the end of March. And flying a kite was something I had learned to do long ago, even with an awkward right arm and leg. So I raced along at the bottom end of a string, with my kite high in the bright blue spring air. And I saw a flight of geese up there too—heading north this early? I thought of Manton, Grandma, the animals, Butch. But they seemed far away and I found that I no longer missed them so much. I was all excited now about training for the Soap Box Derby.

I would have felt better if Patrick had not had Jim's help. I knew Jim would correct Pat's carelessness, and in the end we'd be pretty evenly matched—except for my twin's natural skill at everything and my own natural awkwardness.

Over and over while the other two were making the steering and brake assemblies I examined their work. And time and time again I said, "That ought to be tighter, Jim," or "Your hinges aren't put in very snug, Pat. Let me show you."

Each time Pat said, "Aw, it doesn't show. The main thing is being able to handle the car in the race."

Maybe he was right.

Jimmie and Patrick covered their racer body with

tin plate. First they carefully made a pattern out of brown paper stretched over one half of the car and fastened with thumb tacks. They lapped the pieces over each other about an inch to allow for fitting the sheet-metal panels.

Jim's father was so pleased with Jim that he wanted to get down on his knees and help cut the tin. But Jim said, "Patrick will be disqualified if you do. Just he and I, Dad!"

So his father contented himself with giving Jim the most expensive sample of dark green leather in his stock. And the finished job was really more professional-looking than mine. They painted their tin body dazzling white, with thin stripes of green at the bottom and around the cockpit.

Finally their racer was as finished as I thought it was ever going to be. I knew it was a little careless inside; even though Jim was a good workman, he'd been influenced by Pat's haste. They hadn't bothered to wire their turnbuckles so they couldn't come unwound. And there was that screen-door spring still bothering me. I knew how many dozen times a day that door had been thrown open by some kid wanting to come in and get warm and see how we were coming along with our racers. No, that carelessness I would not have expected of Jim.

One Saturday about the end of March I said at breakfast, "They're finished, Dad. Two racers waiting for the Derby!"

Dad came down into the basement to look them over. Whenever I looked at my racer, my face glowed.

There *was* something magic in the world, after all; I knew it. That magic was creation. At first there had been nothing. Then a pile of junk, a boy who liked to make things, and an idea all came together and produced this little car.

Dad and I bent over mine, admiring it. Suddenly I remembered how we had looked at the insides of the tractor and his other farm machinery together in Smitty's Garage in Manton; and I felt such a beating of love for him I thought my heart would explode.

Then Dad looked at Pat and Jim's car. He went round and round it, and I think he was surprised that Pat could even *help* make anything that neat.

"I'm proud of you both," said Dad. "And may the best man win."

I covered my pretty little car with an old blanket. "That's what I'm afraid of," I said.

Whenever I thought about my racer now, waiting under the old blanket in the basement, I longed to try it out. Yet I dreaded actually putting it to the test. I had made it as carefully as possible, but I feared my ability to drive it. Nevertheless, I could hardly wait for the weather to clear so that I could get it out on that hill in Middle Rouge Park where the races would be held.

Spring came gradually, with many false starts. Even into April the skating pond thawed and froze, thawed and froze again. Hopscotch patterns chalked on sidewalks one day were rained off the next.

The Good Humor truck moved slowly along the drying streets in thin sunlight, jingling its bell. Dare Base

and Run Sheep Run began after supper and lasted until dark.

Betsy and Charlotte and even Emmy Jo jumped rope from early morning until late at night, chanting:

> "By the holy
> Ceremony
> Marry the Indian to the squaw;
> By the blades of my jack knife
> I pronounce you man and wife.
> One, two, three, four. . . ."

The number of times a girl jumped without missing represented the number of children she would have some day.

April days are pretty in Detroit. When a cold winter changes to a melting warm spring filled with bird song, there is joy in the air so great that it bursts like bubbles in a fizzy drink.

As the days began to grow longer I could hang around Whitey's shop later and later before it was dark. Whitey still had to remind me when it was time to go home.

One evening he said, "Mike, suppose I take you and your brother out to Middle Rouge Park this Sunday afternoon to try your racers on Derby Hill."

I felt quivery inside. But when I told Pat he said calmly, "Sure thing."

Whitey came with his pickup just after lunch on Sunday. "Let's weigh you both in your racers," he suggested, "out in my shop."

We took turns sitting in our cars on Whitey's platform scales. My car and I weighed 230 pounds, Patrick with his, just 245.

"Good enough," said Whitey. I wished, as I always did, that just once I could be the heavier twin.

"When you come back from the park," Whitey said, "why don't you both leave your cars in my shop? Then any Saturday or Sunday or evening you want to try them out I'll be glad to take you out to the hill in my pickup."

"I don't want to do that," said Patrick firmly. "I want to keep mine in my own basement."

I felt he was not being very polite to Whitey. "But

will you be here this summer, Whitey?" I asked. "I thought you and your wife would go north for the fishing."

"Not this time, Mike. I've got some extra work around here. And—I wouldn't miss that Derby for the world."

"That's a load off my mind. I don't know how I'd feel if you weren't there, Whitey."

Whitey lifted the two racers one after the other into the pickup and off we went to the park. When we first saw the hill, after dreaming about the race for several months, I was disappointed. It did not look very high.

"Gosh, is that it?" said Patrick, sort of disgusted.

"Just wait," said Whitey. "You have to start from a standstill at the top and let gravity take over. No pushing. It isn't easy to start, and if you haven't enough weight, you can't keep going. There's nine hundred and seventy-five feet to coast down. If you waste one bit by weaving or going out of line, you're through."

We pushed our racers into position at the top of the hill and waited with our brakes down until Whitey called, "One, two, three, go!"

My heart thumped painfully as I saw Pat glide away as gracefully and easily as though he had been racing a car all his life. Straight down the hill he steered, without a thought or doubt in his head, merrily shouting, "Whee-ee-ee!"

My car did not pick up momentum as quickly as Pat's. Once it was started, it came down faster because I was lighter. Then my uneven handling showed up.

My mind told me all kinds of bad news: "You can't even let your brake up as fast as Pat does. Now look how you pull to the left. You'll go clear off the track into the grass in a minute."

And that is just what I did when I was halfway down the hill. I felt like bursting into tears, but I wouldn't give Pat this satisfaction. How awful it was to have my finely constructed car look worse than his! I felt too that I was somehow letting Whitey down.

I scrambled out of my racer and pulled it up to the top of the hill. "Come on, Pat, once more," I begged.

"Okay," Patrick said, grinning.

We swung the cars into place again. Again Whitey counted, "One, two, three, go!"

Again Pat shot out ahead of me before we were halfway down the hill. This time I continued steering straight a little longer. I had a feeling of having mastered my handicap a bit.

"Look, Mike," Patrick said kindly, "you'll have to pull a little extra to your right. Or if you can't pull with your right arm, then use more push in your left. Otherwise you'll be out of the race before they can say, 'Jack Robinson.'"

"I know it."

I made my hands into fists inside my pants pockets. I was just about hating Pat then. Somehow it was worse having him be kind to me than being on the outs the way we had been for a while during the winter.

I tried a third time. This time I felt that while I didn't have the use of some of the right muscles, the others came into use—what do they say, compensated. But I feared my body would forget this lesson before the actual race. I wove my way down to the bottom of the hill many seconds after Pat had got out of his car.

Pat was tired of the sport now. I guess he thought it was no fun always winning. Things came so easily for him. "Let's go home," he said. "There's still time for some baseball before dark."

When we got home Pat joined the other boys playing ball down the street. I sat miserably beside Whitey, unable to speak. Finally Whitey said, "You'll have to practice and practice, Mike."

My eyes were swimming in tears. "Maybe his racer

is better than mine," I muttered. I knew this wasn't true, but I wanted to be reassured.

Whitey stared off up the street, and his blue eyes crinkled at the corners. "You know your racer is as strong and good as possible, Mike. If anything, it may steer a little hard. But you've got to face the fact that your one arm and one leg are crippled. I know you'd rather I didn't say that. But how can you learn to develop the skill you need if you don't admit your weakness? Come on now, Mike. You promised that truant officer last fall that you wouldn't run away from school any more. And you didn't. You can't run away from your problems either."

I rubbed the back of my hand across my eyes. "What can I do about it?" I asked in a low voice.

"I been thinking," he said slowly. "You and I could go to that park every Sunday afternoon from now till the race, and no one would be the wiser."

"But your shop——"

"Oh, I could get a man in to take the pumps, I think. No one but your folks would need to know. How about it?"

I looked gratefully into his long, kind face. "Okay," I said.

Well, it can be told now. All during April we went to that park every Sunday and practiced on Derby Hill. Sometimes glider clubs were flying their gliders in fields near-by. Sometimes picnics were going on under the trees. No one paid much attention to us.

I imagine most people think guiding a racer down

a hill on a sunny spring afternoon is a fine bit of entertainment. It was no entertainment for us though. It
was hard work to me, and to Whitey too. He said, "Now
I'm training you, Mike, just the way an athlete is
trained. You do the same thing over and over until you
know every possible motion and change in position.
Then you do it some more."

I practiced until I was exhausted. Down the hill I
came as straight and fast as possible. Then Whitey,
stopwatch in hand, said quietly, "Again. That was a
couple seconds better."

Each afternoon I would end by being almost angry.
"Can't we go home now?" I'd say.

At the look on Whitey's face I would answer myself,
"No, I guess not. All right, here I go again."

Sometimes I hated my racer. Sometimes I hated
Whitey. Sometimes I hated myself.

And yet, underneath, all the time, I could feel a
growing resolve to win that race. It was not so much
a feeling of competition as it was a need to prove myself and the car I had made so carefully. It deserved
to win.

I guess Whitey would have kept helping me every
weekend till the race started; that's the kind of man
he is. But the man he had on pumps got sick and he
couldn't find anyone else. He couldn't afford not to be
open on Sunday afternoons. So he phoned and told me
one Friday he was sorry, and I said it was okay.

But I was mighty worried with less than two months
to go till the day of the race. I could easily forget all

I'd learned. And I'd lose my self-confidence, which had been coming along slowly.

What happened next you wouldn't believe—but you'll have to take my word that it's honestly, really, cross-my-heart true.

Pat and I

I went down to Mr. Duffy's room on the first of May
to report another "Negative" on my truancy record.
And there was Pat. I was worried and jealous at the
time. Had he got into trouble after all? Or were he and
Mr. Duffy secret pals?

"Patrick and I were just talking about the race," said
Mr. Duffy. "He thinks you need special training to
develop the muscles on your right side. And so do I."

I was so hurt that the tears burst right out of my
eyes, and I fairly yelled, "I don't need your pity. My
muscles are all right."

They both looked shocked and the room was quiet
for what seemed like a whole hour. But it must have
been less than a minute before Mr. Duffy said, "If
anyone pities you, Mike, it's you yourself."

"What do you mean?"

"You're acting as if people who want to help you are
old meanies. Now Pat came to me himself to suggest
we give you some special training. It's not just driving

that car. You'll have to go on living after the Soap Box Derby is over, whether you win or lose."

"*Pat* suggested helping me? It wasn't your idea?" I had supposed again that Mr. Duffy was trying to protect me.

"You've been going out to try your racer every Sunday afternoon with Whitey," said Pat. I had thought he didn't know; try to keep a secret from your twin and see how far you get. "How's it coming?"

I flopped down on the nearest chair, made my hands into fists, and beat the knuckles together. "Not so good," I said miserably. "And Whitey told me Friday he can't go out any more; he has to man his gas pumps all the time. Oh, Patrick," I wailed suddenly, "what'll I do? I don't know why you should want to help me when you're gonna race against me."

Pat looked out of the window and I looked too and saw some nice egg-white clouds scudding by, way up in the blue. "I want to help you, Mike," he said, "because it's no sport racing against someone you know darn well you can beat. A race is no fun unless it's really close."

Well, that was honest enough, and I'd asked for it.

"Patrick's right," said Mr. Duffy. "And there is a lot we can do to help you. I'm just so proud two of my boys are going to be in the Derby I'll help every way I can."

"It really isn't fair Jim can't drive that car," I said, a little sullen still. I wasn't giving in too easily. "He did all the hard work on it. You just took orders, and sometimes you didn't carry them out very carefully."

"Well, okay, so I'm a stinker."

"Oh, I'm sorry, Patrick, honest I am. I guess Jim's used to being the fat boy just like I'm used to being called a screwball."

"Now, no more of that, Mike," said Mr. Duffy, sternly. "Cut that out entirely. Your brother came in here to offer to help you build your muscle tone, and we were going to suggest it as carefully as we could. But maybe you don't deserve to be helped if you take the attitude that everything is someone else's fault and people are just going around calling you names."

"Come on, Mike, wouldn't it be fun to work together?"

Pat sounded kind of lonesome. And it suddenly dawned on me that when we were on the outs he felt just as bad about it as I did. When you're twins, you're different from others, see? You can almost feel each other's feelings and share each other's thoughts. And if you're sore at each other or not getting along for some reason, it's like each of you was split down the middle, not whole, not right.

When Pat made up his mind to something he sure went into it whole-hog. He never let up on me after I'd agreed to try to develop my right arm and leg muscles. If I flopped down on the floor after school to read the afternoon paper, he'd bring out Dad's bowling ball and say, "Sit on a straight chair while you read and let this hang down from your right hand."

"Are you crazy?"

"No. Mr. Duffy talked to the school doctor. He gave us a whole lot of things to try. You've protected those

weaker muscles instead of using them. Now you'll
have to give that up."

I'd been protecting myself, or part of myself! Well,
that was a new switch. Here I'd been blaming everyone else when I thought they over-protected me. With
a sigh, I sat on a straight chair and held that heavy
bowling ball till suppertime. Oh, it didn't take me that
long to read the headlines and the funnies; but Patrick
made me keep holding it even when I watched television.

At night when we went to bed I'd lie flat and Pat
would massage my right leg, grabbing into the muscles, saying, "Feel that? Is it sore? Well, *good*."

I knew, because he explained what the school doctor
had told Mr. Duffy, that pain was better than numb-
ness. If there was any life in a muscle, there was a
chance of its being revived, gradually built up, caused
to grow strong. Maybe I don't use the right terms, but
that's about it, anyway.

"Why didn't we do all these things before?" I asked
once.

And Pat said, sharp-like: "Because we didn't know
about them. These are things the doctors are trying,
but they don't know when they'll work and when they
won't. Now turn over, lie on your back; that's the way."

He consulted a chart someone had given him, and
suddenly plunged his hand into a whole new area of
muscle and nerve. I nearly hit the ceiling. "Hey, look
out."

"Good." He sounded real pleased with himself. "I'm

glad that hurt. Maybe I could learn to be a—what do you call it?—an osteopath."

While he was kneading muscles so that every so often my leg jerked a little he said, "Wonder what ever became of that Little Atlas Muscle Builder we had on the farm. Remember?"

"Yeah. I remember hating it. Especially when you got so good at pulling the pulleys that the weights went clear up to the ceiling. I guess the folks gave it away."

"But the weightlifting is good, Mike, so you keep at it."

"Oh, sure—the old bowling ball, I know."

The things we did inside the house, where the other kids couldn't watch, weren't so bad. But when Pat told me he could teach me to bat a ball I rebelled. "Not for a while, Patrick," I begged. "I can't stand to be made fun of. I can still hear those kids yelling, 'Screwball.' "

"Well, okay, but we can do some pitch and catch. Come on."

He'd throw a nice easy ball, and for every time that I caught it there would be eight or nine times that it dropped when my arm didn't come up in time. At first he got real mad, said I wasn't half trying, and we went home sore at each other.

But something had happened to Pat, I could feel it. He liked me again. So he talked about the ball games to Mr. Duffy, who said, "Keep them up. Keep a score. See if he improves."

One day after gym class, when we had run around the gym about fifty times and my legs felt as if they would give way beneath me, I panted out, "Mr. Duffy, isn't there any danger of over-stretching my muscles?"

He laughed hard. "What's the matter, Mike, you want to quit?"

He knew I didn't. But I wondered often what was the use of all this self-torture. I had little hope of not being lopsided all my life. And I still don't know now whether we did my muscles any special good. It was probably never any use expecting I'd get back to normal. It didn't even really help my confidence in myself very much. But it made a wonderful patch of friendship between Pat and me.

Then there were all the sessions of driving my racer up and down our street, with Pat pushing. Every day after school Pat made me go several times around the block, guiding my car, while he and the other guys took turns pushing me. And you know, it's a funny thing—I began not minding getting all that attention for what I'd always secretly thought of as my "weakness." They were all so determined that the two boys from their school should put up a good race that I didn't feel all trembly and ashamed when I ran off the sidewalk on my right side and someone yelled, "Now watch that, Mike, you're not trying."

"Like fun I'm not. Come on, Winslow, your turn to give me a push."

Oh, they made Patrick try out his racer around the block too. But he always stayed exactly on course, so there wasn't much worry over him.

On Saturday and Sunday afternoons during May Dad took us out to Middle Rouge Park to try both our

cars on Derby Hill. That was fun too, because spring
in a Detroit park can be a pretty thing. Charlotte came
along in our car, and she and Betsy found some little
flowers they called "spring beauties" under dead leaves
down in a ravine.

They were tiny and pink with darker pink veins—no
smell though, and of course not as wonderful as the
arbutus around Manton, but the kids loved finding
them. And violets! One Saturday there were about a
million; by the next weekend they were all gone. Too
many people, people like Betsy and Charlotte, who just
couldn't leave wild flowers alone.

Mom always took wieners or the makings for hamburgers and we parked our car by one of the outdoor
grills. Dad made a fire with charcoal, and after we'd
tried out our racers till it was almost dark Mom would
sing out, "Come and get it." And to Dad she'd say,
"The mosquitoes are out. Hope you brought that spray
can."

It would all have been most wonderful fun, except
that well over half the times we raced downhill Pat
won. I tried to study his technique of driving. Sometimes I refused to go down when he did but stood
watching instead. And what I never got over marveling
at was his pure self-confidence.

He had the same simple, natural skill at using his
whole body that a good hunter has in hitting his
target. You've heard of an archer who can shoot an
arrow at his mark without taking aim more than just
for a single instant. I've read about one who doesn't
even look where he's aiming; he can hit a bull's-eye

in the dark. He knows where he wants the arrow to go, and he sends it there.

That was the way Patrick was with his car. He just got in, not tense, not even seeming to care one way or the other. He waited for Dad's signal, just as I was waiting—except that I was as tense as a coiled spring, crouched over the cut-out V in the top of my steering wheel as if my life depended on getting down to the bottom of that hill first. Well, if my life had depended on it, I would have died time after time while Patrick sailed down as easy as pie and waited for me almost every time for a couple of seconds at least.

Other boys were sometimes out there too, getting groomed for the big race. I could feel the excitement in the air, and I'd see them steal glances at our cars and look down at their own, wondering which was going to be the best when the big day came.

Jim came along with us once, but he was pretty busy now with his paper route. His dad had finally agreed Jim needed to earn some money of his own. After watching us go down half a dozen times, Jim was pretty sure if either Pat or I placed in the finals, it would be Pat. He looked kind of sorry for me, I thought, when Pat beat me down to the foot of the hill four times out of six. He didn't say much at the time.

But in the last week of May he came into the basement one evening when I was tinkering over my racer. I couldn't stay away from it. I didn't believe in myself as a driver, but I sure believed in that little car. "Hi, Mike," said Jim, "saw the light on down here and hoped it was you."

"Why?"

"Well—gosh—I've been reading over the rule book for the Derby, and I'm just afraid our car might be disqualified, Mike. Pat's and mine, I mean."

I sat back on my heels and looked up at him. For a second, that seemed to me a pretty nice idea. Suppose their car was disqualified for safety reasons, I'd sure stand a better chance in the race. The next second, I was ashamed of this thought. Here was Pat helping me so I could race him without making a fool of myself. And here was I thinking how good it would be if he happened not to pass the preliminary inspection of our cars!

"Gee, whiz, Jim, that would be terrible, wouldn't it?" I said. "And hard on you after all the work you've gone to."

"Sure would." Jim took a candy bar out of his pants pocket, unwrapped it, and bit a large bite to console himself. He held it out toward me, but I shook my head. I was too excited these days to eat much.

"Pat's been so nice helping me. Maybe I could help him a little, eh?" I said thoughtfully.

"That's what I been thinking. Maybe you and I could go over my car—oh, I mean his, of course—and true it up. We were careless every step of the way, Mike, and I know it.

"My Dad was lecturing me last night about responsibility. He thinks it's pretty swell that I've taken a paper route, even if he wouldn't let me this winter; and we've been talking about saving my money and all that. And he said, 'Whatever you do, whatever you make, be sure you can be proud of it afterwards.'

"And, golly, I thought about how Pat and I fudged on our racer so we'd get through. We were more careful about the paint job and upholstering and outside trim than we were about the steering assembly."

"Well, Pat's been demonstrating that the thing steers straight as an arrow, Jim. But I know what you mean. Something might go wrong at the last minute if you haven't been as careful as you should've been. Let's look her over."

Lucky for us Pat was over at Emmy Jo's studying for a social studies final. So we had that whole evening to go over the racer.

I was shocked when we looked at the inside of that car, using a flash light to see each detail. It's hard to explain everything that was just slightly wrong: The hinges to one front bulkhead hadn't been screwed in real tight, since Jim had left that for Pat to do. The axle bolts to the axletree were so loose I could twist them with my fingers! And, of course, the turnbuckles hadn't been wired tight to keep them from loosening. Little things, but important.

Point by point we went over the steering assembly, trueing up everything, and while we were at it, making it what Whitey Jones calls "eye sweet," so the inspectors before the prelims wouldn't throw it out as a careless job.

We didn't get to the brake assembly that night. We were scared to work on it too long for fear Pat would see the basement light on and come in. Mom always made him come home by ten.

"The first chance we get," I said, as we pulled a piece of canvas over the pretty little green-and-white car, "we've got to change that screen-door spring you're using to hold up the brake. You know those things have only so much life in them before they begin to stretch."

"Yeah, maybe you're right, though it looks strong and tight."

"Sure. Take a look at me, Jim. You'd never know that my right muscles are weaker than my left, would you?"

He shook his head. "How's it coming, Mike? Think you're improving?"

I couldn't nod or shake my head because I didn't honestly know. I stood there looking miserable. Then I brightened.

"Well, if I don't improve, it's not Pat's fault anyway. He's giving it all he's got."

"Sure is."

We waited day after day, hoping for a chance to get to that brake assembly. I even went to a hardware store one afternoon and bought a good, tight, new, shiny black-painted screen-door spring to put in, in place of the used one. I thought our chance would never come. Either Pat was with me, training me like a professional athlete getting ready for some big contest, or he was with Jim and Hubert down at the tree house, each kidding the others about Emmy Jo Thompson.

Then I really got worried; so I told Dad our problem. "He's been such a help to me, Dad, I want his racer to be first-rate too. Jim and I went all over the steering assembly. It's as good as we can make it now. And every so often I get a minute by myself to check over the brake; but honest, I don't feel right about it."

Dad grinned. "Seems to me each of you wants the other to win."

"You know that isn't so. We just want to be good competition for each other. It's no fun winning otherwise."

"Sure. Sure, I know. Well, I'll ask Pat to go bowling with me this evening, and you and Jim can get to work then."

"Swell. Thanks a million."

I counted on him. So did Jim. But this time Pat turned Dad down. He didn't want to go away from our street. It was a warm evening, and he'd seen Emmy Jo sitting with Mildred Lucile on the McMurtries' front porch.

And from there I guess he saw our basement light on. Jim and I were bent over his racer just getting ready to unfasten the old screen-door spring and put in the new one when Pat came through the door from the driveway.

"What are you guys doing?" he yelled. "Get away from my racer, Mike!" He came in swinging his arms as if he wanted to swat me one. "This all you care about me trying to help you?"

I wanted to explain, but he didn't give me a chance. I could see he was mad clear through. Jim said reasonably, "Calm down, Pat. We're just gonna put a new spring on for the brake. Mike bought one for you."

"Like fun, you do!" He came over, grabbed the new spring, and threw it so hard it hit the opposite wall and fell into the ash can. When I fished it out later, it didn't look so good as the old spring that was already fastened into the racer. And Pat never let me get that close to his car again.

"But, Pat—"

"Never you mind. This is the thanks I get for helping you."

"But you don't know how important . . . you don't——"

"All I know is you're jealous. You want credit for making my racer better. Says you. I keep telling you it's the driving that counts. And you'd better be lifting weights and doing knee bends and those exercises I gave you. And *let my racer alone!*"

He looked so fierce that I backed away and Jim said quietly, "Okay, Pat, I think Mike's been too worried about that anyway. That spring is okay, I'm sure."

"Well, just let him worry about his driving. I'll take care of my end of this race. You keep hands off this car, hear?" He put the canvas over it, jammed his fists into his pockets, and went out.

Well, as I've said all along, twins are funny. Add them together and divide by two to find what each one is like. I just crossed my fingers and hoped Pat's car would pass inspection. I still wanted to race him, not just every other boy in Detroit.

I wanted to race my twin—and win. But I didn't think I was likely to.

The Soap Box Derby

The last day of school came, as it always does when boys have about given up hope.

Mr. Duffy burned my truancy record as he had promised me, and we shook hands above his wastebasket. I'm not kidding you. He said, "We pulled off a perfect report, Mike. It's been a pleasure seeing you once a month in my office. How do you feel about the Derby now?"

"Well, I don't know. I guess I've got a chance."

"Sure you have."

"And I'll never forget how everyone helped me, especially Patrick."

For days kids swarmed the street on bicycles, scooters, and roller skates; and I went back to pulling the little kids on my old coaster when Patrick and I weren't working out our racers. But for a day or so we were tired of them, along with everything that had to do with the past months of school.

We went down to our tree house and swept out the

dead leaves and built a bench along one side. We decided to make a set of Tree House Club rules. Jim's dad gave us a new piece of material for a curtain, this time bright green.

We made a fire in an empty lot that wasn't empty enough, and the fire department came to put it out. Dickie Fells wandered out beyond Eight Mile Road and his nervous old grandmother called the police. They brought him home and he wouldn't speak to his grandmother for the rest of the day. We guys sat on front porches and I listened while the other fellows argued about famous athletes.

They were tired of baseball for a few days, the way I was tired of thinking about the race. But by and by they teamed up again for the summer, and Pat and I filled out entry blanks for the Soap Box Derby.

One day in June we received engraved formal dinner invitations in heavy white envelopes. Up and down the street flew the news, and all the kids were almost as excited as we were.

We were guests at a hotel dinner for all the boys who were to be in the Derby, almost three hundred with their fathers or sponsors. We listened to speeches about sportsmanship, and each boy was given a white steel helmet to keep until the day of the race.

We Williamses got a lot of publicity because we were the only twins competing against each other. We even had our picture in the papers. Pat looked very confident and handsome, and I was ducking my head and grinning a bit.

Now came the preliminary tryouts, a week before the Derby. These would eliminate two thirds of the entrants. Pat and I, bathed and combed as never before, sat together on the front steps of our house.

The scattered showers that had been promised whispered among the elm leaves. But the big drops did no more than settle the dust and bring out a smell of dryness before the sun was shining again.

Whitey came before one o'clock, put the racers in the back of his pickup, and we scrambled into the seat beside him.

"What if we're both eliminated today?" said Pat, beginning at last, I guess, to feel butterflies in his stomach.

"What if you win today and I don't?" I added. This seemed much more likely to me.

"The heats will be run off three cars at a time," said Whitey. "I've been reading the rules in the paper."

At the park, the grandstands for the Derby were being set up. The noise of hammers filled the air, and the men in charge were in work clothes.

"These your racers?" said one. "Let's weigh you in."

I looked with interest at all the other homemade cars. Pat pushed his racer onto the scales and climbed in.

"Two hundred and forty-three," said the man, who was writing down the entries.

I weighed in at two hundred and thirty-one, and the checker said, "Little light there, sonny. Better eat some beans before next Saturday."

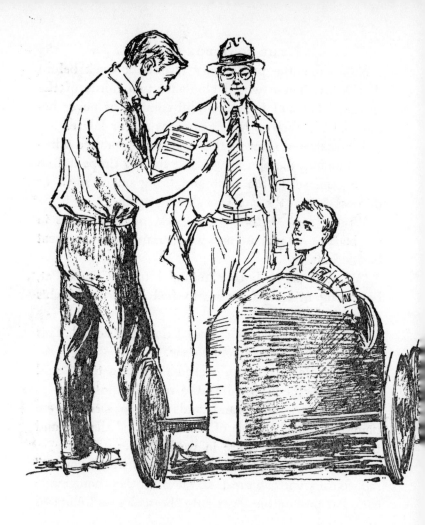

No one seemed to take these first run-offs very seriously. Men in shirt sleeves sat at a table with check lists in front of them, while two men inspected the cars.

The inspection was so thorough that I was worried,

especially for Pat. I felt that my racer was as pretty inside as outside. But I'd got so eager to improve Pat's car maybe I'd missed some detail on my own.

Two men checked our expense lists, while another two went rapidly over the cars. They checked the way the kingpin had been put in. They turned the front axles to measure the play of the wheels. They peered inside to see how the steering cable had been wound. They checked the turnbuckles to see that they had been properly wired so they wouldn't unlock. They tipped forward the hinged seat-backs in the cockpits and examined the brake mechanisms. But they couldn't tell that Pat's spring, suspended from the bulkhead, was a used one. I breathed more easily when they didn't notice. Pat looked at me and shrugged.

I thought the inspection would never end. I felt wound up tight inside. "Got to be sure they're safe," one of the men explained.

And he continued to check the wheels, run his thumb over the tires, and poke and pry until Pat laughed, "Gee, you'd think we had stolen these cars instead of making them."

Finally both our racers were accepted and we stood in a new line, while a man looked up our names. "Williams, hm? Two Williamses. Twins, eh? That's a new one. Oh, yeah, saw your picture in the paper. Well, today you're separated. I don't know how it'll be next week. Mike, you're paired off with Watson and Weisenfels. Pat, let's see here—you're with Warren and Yarnell. Stick around and be ready when you're called."

It seemed a long time before the starter called, "Patrick Williams, Warren, and Yarnell to the starting line."

Pat and two other boys ran forward and brought their racers into place at the top of the hill. One of the cars was a crude boxlike affair and the other a bright red job covered with barrel staves.

I stood with my hands in my pockets, trying honestly to want Patrick to win. The hill was the exact length of the racing distance at Derby Downs in Akron, 975.4 feet long.

"Next Saturday there will be a starter bar to nose your racers up against," said the starter. "But today you hold your feet on your brakes till I give the signal. Then sit still and let gravity take over. When I drop the flag, that means, 'Let her go.'"

He dropped the flag, and the boys released their feet from the brakes. Warren's boxlike racer started to weave almost at once, and before he was a third of the way it had gone completely out of control. He had to steer it over to one side and drop out of the race.

I could not look at him. I knew how he must be feeling.

The other two cars continued as one. Patrick had real steering control. His wheels never once touched the lane lines. Yarnell could drive too, but Pat had the edge. I could see the triumphant grin on his face as he nosed ahead slowly—ever so slowly—and finished a half length ahead of the other boy.

My heart felt big inside my throat. Now it was up to me to get into the finals too. I felt that nothing else would ever be so important.

It was almost four o'clock before someone called, "Now for the last heat of the day—Watson, Mike Williams, Weisenfels."

Someone whispered in the man's ear, and he bent sidewise to hear. "What's that? He was? Okay. Sorry, folks, Watson has been eliminated."

Poor guy, I thought.

Later, on the way home, Patrick told me the inspectors had suspected for some reason that the boy's father had helped him. And when they asked him he broke down and admitted his dad had done a good part of the work.

The Weisenfels boy and I lined up at the top of the hill. He surveyed my orange car calmly, then looked down at his own. He had fitted lath strips evenly over the entire body and painted every other one charcoal gray; the alternate strips were painted light gray. I have to admit it was one of the smartest finish jobs in the park. No wonder he looked proud.

"Let her go."

I had not expected the signal quite so soon. I kept my foot on the brake just a fraction of a second too long, and the Weisenfels boy got away down the hill a foot or two ahead of my car.

Then he did a foolish thing. I can hardly bear to think how I would have fared if he hadn't done it. He was more than halfway down, and he thought he had nothing more to worry about. So he turned slightly toward me and waved his hand. In that second his car swerved out of line. I'm sure he could have righted it instantly except that he must have made his steering cable too tight. The mechanism was too rigid for fingertip control. Another moment and I had passed him!

It seemed many minutes to me before I got up any kind of speed. I dared not look at the car behind me, but I could hear it, and it did not seem to be gaining on me.

I was going fast now, fast enough to make me think of the brake, and to reject the thought. I had lost a little of my steering control since the last time I practiced. Maybe I was too scared. If my right arm slacked up on me, good night!

I felt myself leaning to the right, "wishing" my racer back onto the guide line. Then I overshot the line and was panicky for fear of a steering failure.

The car did steer hard. As steering friction was overcome by tight muscles, it would suddenly turn, and I would over-steer. So my path to the finish line was not quite so straight as a string. But if it was not the shortest distance between two points it was at least fast enough. I crossed the line a full length ahead of Weisenfels.

I thought afterwards that I had counted every one of those 975 feet, and that it was only on the seven hundredth I had passed my opponent—too close for comfort.

At any rate, I had passed him, and the race for that day at least was decided. Both Pat and I would compete again next Saturday in the Derby. Altogether eighty-one boys made the prelims and qualified for the final race.

When Whitey let us out at our house, I said, "Listen, Whitey, I'll be out tomorrow and check over my car with you if that's okay. There's something wrong with every single bit of it."

Pat looked puzzled, but Whitey nodded. He and I understood each other. He knew that I had to tinker with my racer, even if I took the whole thing apart and put it together again worse than it was before.

All the next week I spent most of my time doing what Pat called "fooling around" with my car. A little adjustment here, a turn of a turnbuckle there, wheels off in front, then back on again, and testing, testing, testing for control, for steerability, for brake efficiency. It was all fun, no matter what the result might be. But I knew too—especially since the preliminaries—how important to me the race had become.

On the Saturday of the Derby the street was seething with excitement. I thought if anyone touched me, I would give off sparks! Every family packed a picnic basket. Larry, Richard, Hubert, and Jim had made a pennant saying, "Pat and Mike," in the Pontchartrain School colors of blue and gold. They fastened it across the back of the McMurtries' car, which was the biggest on the block.

Charlotte had curled her hair in honor of the big event. She gave me her Music Club pin to wear. I'm sure I turned red when she fastened the gold treble clef on my tie, but it made me happy.

"You ride with my folks," I told her.

"Of course," she said.

Pat and I went with Whitey in his pickup so we could be near our racers.

The park was all dressed up with flags and decorations. Bands played and thousands of people from all over Detroit filled the grandstands. There were slick big programs for sale. Whitey bought one and pointed out, "Look, here are your names—Michael Williams; Patrick Williams. It's the first time, I think, that there have been twins in the Derby."

"Maybe." Pat was quieter than I'd ever seen him, no fizz or sparkle at all. "Here comes Mr. Duffy."

Sure enough, Mr. Duffy was there. He came up beside us, with his wife and two little girls, enough like him to make you want to laugh. For once he was all dressed up.

He grabbed my hand and said, "You just forget I was ever your truant officer, won't you, Mike?"

"I'll never forget who sent us both a Derby Rule Book for Christmas," I said.

Pat grinned and said, "Me neither, Mr. Duffy."

"Well, today one of you will go farther than the other. But whatever happens, remember you're both important people in the world."

"Sure, sure." Pat knew he was important and laughed as if Mr. Duffy was making a joke. But I turned and watched till he was out of sight as he moved off to find grandstand seats for his family.

We were on the grassy hilltop among the other contestants. I wondered if they all felt as tightly wound as I did. Whitey sat down for a minute beside us, mumbling the words printed on the back of the program: "True sportsmanship is one of America's grandest traditions, and one of her greatest needs for the future. The Soap Box Derby has taught thousands of boys not only the joys of creative work, the benefits of inventiveness, and the value of resourcefulness, but also the even more important lesson of fair play." He read slowly, pushing at the words with one finger, darkened by years of work on greasy engines.

I looked at him nervously. I knew he meant well, but this was no time for a pep talk. Whitey stood up and said, "Well, guess I'll find Amy and the kid. See you after the race."

"Yeah, Whitey." I didn't turn my head when he walked away into the crowd.

Suddenly a loudspeaker gargled, then spoke in a voice that hushed the chatter all over the park: "Ladies and gentlemen, welcome to Detroit's annual Soap Box Derby. Today's race will be run in four rounds. In the first round there are twenty-seven heats. This means that, for twenty-seven times, three cars will race down the hill—eighty-one cars altogether.

"From each of these heats will come a winner. The twenty-seven boys winning first round will race, three at a time, in nine heats, making the second round. From this second round there will be, then, nine winners.

"In the third round there will be only three heats of three racers each. And in the fourth and final round, of course, the three winners from the third round will compete."

The first few heats seemed to go on forever, although each took less than a minute. I saw that Pat's first heat came ahead of mine, and I waited impatiently for it to begin.

Pat made his way to the top of the hill a long time

before his heat was called. There was such a crush of boys and I was so short I could not see the heat when Pat's name, as one of three, was finally announced.

But presently I heard over the loudspeaker, "Winner in the twelfth heat, Patrick Williams."

The heats went on and on and finally I was at the top of the hill, one of three in white helmets. I grinned tightly at nobody in particular—at everybody, I suppose—and kept tense hands on my steering wheel. I could not see my family or Whitey or Mr. Duffy, and I did not want to.

I could think of nothing except this racer I had made. My nerves tingled and my muscles were tense. I felt as if my whole right side was a little numb. But in spite of that, I felt as sure as I could feel that I would win this first heat.

I was ready this time the instant the flag dropped. When I released the brake I also released the tension in me. All the things Pat and the others had done to help me were at work, and I glided down like a bird headed for its nest. It was all over in a fraction more than thirty-two seconds. My car was down at the red finish flag, and the announcer was saying at the microphone: "The winner of the seventeenth heat in the first round is Mickey—correction, Mike—Williams."

The heats went on in a blur of confusion. Presently all of the first twenty-seven were completed. Now the field was narrowed to a total of twenty-seven boys instead of eighty-one. I began to be more and more excited.

I wished I could push back time. It was going too fast. How would I face all our friends if in the second round Pat won and I did not?

There was time to move around and get cold drinks before the second round began. For once Pat and I stuck together. We knew we should look up the family, but Pat said he felt calmer not knowing where they were and I agreed.

Scores of the audience had gone home after the first round, taking their defeated entries. The crowd now was smaller but far more keyed up over the nine heats to come. We boys waiting to race could feel the tension of the audience as if it came to us in waves from the grandstand. This, added to our own, made us fit to explode, I tell you.

The announcer said, "Ladies and gentlemen, starting now the second round of the afternoon. The names of the contestants will be drawn by chance from this revolving drum by little Miss Shirley Roth."

A girl with long curls and long thin legs under stiff pink skirts stood beside him. She drew out three slips of paper and the man read, "Robert Parr, Gerald Whitmire, Patrick Williams."

Almost at once the three cars were there in line behind the starting bar at the top of the hill. The starter waited for silence and attention before dropping the flag. He kept in perfect time with the man who released the starting bar.

These three cars were far better matched than earlier sets. They started fairly even and stayed even as they gained speed. I was chewing my nails; it looked to me as though a dead heat was in prospect. But no, one car was dropping behind—a white car with green trim—Pat's.

I couldn't understand it at first. Then I guessed the trouble. Pat's drag brake was bobbing up and down rhythmically, grazing the ground on each swing. That spring had finally lost some of its tightness. The inches of lost ground added up to feet, and Pat finished a half length behind the second car, a lame third at the finish flag.

Poor guy! If only he had let me put in the new spring when I had started to! That was a bad mistake, I thought. But I'll never say, "I told you so."

I could scarcely believe that he was through, finished. I felt a mixture of sorrow and relief that was hard to endure. Pat stood by himself watching the winner being surrounded by friends. He had dragged his car to one side when I joined him. I asked myself what chance I had now of winning and it seemed pretty slim. For had not Patrick beaten me almost every time we had raced for practice? His defeat shook me badly.

"Sorry, Patrick," I said. And I really was.

Pat hit me below the shoulder blades. "Mike, now you try real hard," he said, sobbing. "You try for our school, and all of us, Mike. Try."

It was funny that he should urge me to try. Naturally I would try!

I was in the final heat of the second round. Something about winning my first heat had given me a sense of command of this old hill. I started down as confidently as Patrick used to do when we raced together.

In a matter of seconds, seconds packed tight with speed, the announcer was saying, "And the winner in the final heat of the second round is Mike—this time I know how to pronounce it—Mike Williams. Intermission now, for fifteen minutes."

This time the family found us. Mr. and Mrs. Hoyt and several plump cousins and Jim and Hubert came too. They were all surrounding Pat to tell him it didn't matter that he had lost. What else could they say?

And of course they were by now all rooting for me, since Pat was through. Whitey came too and stood around behind the others grinning his old horse-faced grin, sort of foolish but fond. He didn't say anything; Whitey had done all he could for me.

Mr. Duffy showed up a minute before intermission was over. "Keep cool now, Mike," he said, taking me aside. "Only three heats this next round. You're going great. You drive that car as if you had every muscle in your arms and legs named and could call on them to do what you want."

I smiled and didn't say a word. I didn't want to waste my breath.

Dad gripped my shoulder hard, but he didn't say anything. He kept his arm around Pat's shoulder—just touching, though, no big comforting act.

There were many delays before the semi-finals were run, but I was lucky this time. Mine was the first name drawn. And again I won the heat I was in. Now I would be one of the three finalists!

I had made it almost all the way. I felt as if I were really and truly sitting on top of the world when the last race of the day, the Derby final for Detroit, began.

I looked out calmly across the crowd into trees that were turning gold with late sun. I felt that I and the orange racing car I had made were now one mechanism. I had tested it many, many times under stress, and I believed in it. It had become more important than myself.

But I believed in myself now too.

I must not let this little car down by any faults in steering or control. My left hand fingered the pin Charlotte had given me to wear. Then I brought my hand down to the steering wheel just in time, for—

The flag was down!

This time I was in the middle lane, the trickiest of the three, where my right-sided weakness might get me into trouble.

The cars began to roll. I was choked with a surge of fright as I saw the boys on both sides get slightly ahead. The blood was singing in my ears. The trees were a green blur. I leaned forward anxiously.

And then, suddenly, I knew the tremendous experience of having the thing I had made take hold of me and go of its own accord. I was merely the pilot of a mechanism that, it seemed to me, had its own will. From then on, my steering was entirely unconscious. I did the right things because each moment demanded them.

And just as, in the preliminary tryout, I had felt that I passed my opponent at the seven hundredth foot, so today at almost exactly that same point I saw the boy on my left drop behind. Then, not more than a dozen

feet before I reached the goal, I passed the boy on my right.

And the little orange-pumpkin car, maybe not the most beautiful outwardly but surely the most perfect mechanically, shot its nose over the finish line!

What was all the roaring? Why, it was the noise of victory. I had never heard it for myself before. The crowd was standing, shouting, screaming. The race was over. I, Michael Williams, had won the Detroit Soap Box Derby.

I sat, unable to get out of my car, while people closed in around me. Pat was there, and although the tears started again when he dashed up to me, he was shouting, "Mike, you did it!"

Mr. Hoyt was clasping his plump hands above his head in congratulation. His wife, blowing her nose and wiping red eyes, waved to me from among the happy people crowding from all directions. You'd have thought the gang from our street had believed all along that I was to be the champion. Every guy who'd ever yelled, "Screwball," was there reaching out to shake my hand.

The man with the microphone was holding it over the heads of the crowd shouting, "Say something to your public, Michael."

So I yelled, "Hi, everybody—Mom, Dad, Bets, Pat, Charlotte, Larry, Richard, Hubert, Jim, Whitey. Thanks, everyone." Then just as he was taking the mike away I grabbed it in my hand and yelled, "Wait a minute. I want to say a special thanks to the truant officer of the Pontchartrain School. Thanks, Mr. Duffy."

Gee, they laughed in roars, everyone, as if I'd made a big joke.

I got out of the car and men lifted me to their shoulders and carried me to the edge of the crowd. I knew that my car would be taken by the committee and shipped to Akron, where in a short while I would try my luck against far bigger odds than today's.

I knew a great many things in those few moments while the men were carrying me on their shoulders. I knew that it would never again matter so much to me whether I won or lost a race. I might not win the finals in Akron, though I would try. But win or lose at Akron, you know you are one of the best.

The big thing was that, finally, I knew myself that I was okay. That is what I had been missing all the time. It was not other people I had had to prove my worth to; I had had to prove it to myself. I knew now that I could be a real mechanic some day, a really good one.

Mr. Duffy had said, "You'll have to go on living after

the Derby is over, whether you win or lose. . . . Whatever happens, remember you're both important people in the world." Looking out over the crowd of happy faces, I was sure I would never forget his words.

I struggled to get down from the men's shoulders. I pushed through the circle of reporters, who were asking for my address and my ambition and my middle name.

I ran forward to my family. Dad was the first to throw his arms around me. I was gulping some tears, which surprised me. For why should I have any tears when for the first time in my life I felt completely confident?

"Oh, Mike," said Charlotte, "when we get home will you sign my autograph book?"

"Better wait and see if I win in Akron first," I said.

"Good work, Michael," said Patrick.

And I realized that never before had he used my full name.